2005

# THE HOWARDS OF CAXLEY

Portway Large Print

Published by us ~
chosen by you

# THE HOWARDS OF CAXLEY

## MISS READ

A Portway Large Print Book

PUBLISHED BY
Remploy Press, Halifax

First published in 1967
by
Michael Joseph Ltd

© Miss Read 1967

Published in large print 1994
by arrangement with
Michael Joseph Ltd

*The right of Miss Read to be identified as the author
of this work has been asserted by her in accordance with
the Copyright, Designs and Patents Act 1988*

ISBN 0 7066 1054 7

All rights reserved. No part of this publication may be reproduced,
stored in a retrieval system, or transmitted, in any form or by any
means, electronic, mechanical, photocopying, recording or otherwise,
without the prior permission of the publishers.

This Large Print Edition is published
by Remploy Ltd in association
with Library Services Ltd, a
Library Association Company.

Typeset and Printed by
Page Bros, Norwich
Bound by Remploy Ltd
Halifax

# CONTENTS

## Part One
## 1939–1945

| | |
|---|---:|
| Happy Independence | 1 |
| The Shadow of War | 13 |
| Evacuees in Caxley | 22 |
| War Breaks Out | 35 |
| Grim News | 49 |
| Edward in Love | 63 |
| The Market Square Again | 75 |
| The Invasion | 88 |
| Edward and Angela | 101 |
| Victory | 113 |

## Part Two
## 1945–1950

| | |
|---|---:|
| Edward Starts Afresh | 129 |
| A Family Tragedy | 142 |
| New Horizons | 159 |
| Interlude in Ireland | 170 |
| Edward and Maisie | 185 |
| Harvest Loaves | 198 |
| Problems for Edward | 210 |
| Edward Meets His Father | 222 |
| Return to the Market Square | 235 |
| John Septimus Howard | 246 |

*To Pat and John with love*

# Part One
# 1939–1945

## HAPPY INDEPENDENCE

It was six o'clock on a fine May morning.

The market square was deserted. Long shadows lay across the cobblestones, reaching almost to the steps of St Peter's church. Pink sunlight trembled across its old grey stone, gilding the splendid spire and warming the hoary saints in their niches. A thin black cat, in a sheltered angle of the porch, washed one upthrust leg, its body as round and curved as an elegant shell. Not even the pigeons disturbed its solitude, for they still slept, roosting in scores on the ledges of the Corn Exchange and the Victorian Town Hall.

A hundred yards away, the river Cax, swollen with spring rains, swept in a shining arc through the buttercup fields. The haze of early hours lay over all the countryside which surrounded the little market town, veiling the motionless clumps of elm trees in the fields and the cottages still sleeping among their dewy gardens.

The minute hand of St. Peter's clock began its

slow downhill journey from the gilded twelve, and Edward Howard, pyjama-clad at his bedroom window near by, watched it with mounting exhilaration. This was the life! How wonderful to be alive on such a morning, to be twenty-one and – best of all – to have a place of one's own!

He flung up the window and leaned out, snuffing the morning air like a young puppy. The sun touched his face with gentle warmth. It was going to be a real scorcher, he thought to himself happily. He laughed aloud and the thin cat, arrested in the midst of its toilet, gazed up at him, a tongue as pink as a rose petal still protruding from its mouth.

'Good morning!' called Edward civilly to the only other waking inhabitant of the market square. The cat stared at him disdainfully, shrugged, and then continued with its washing.

And Edward, turning towards the bathroom, followed its good example.

Lying in warm water, he ran an appraising eye round the bathroom and mused upon his good fortune. At this time last year he had been living at Rose Lodge, a mile away on the hill south of Caxley, with his mother and grandmother North. It had been his home for seven or eight years, and he had, he supposed, been reasonably happy there in the company of the two women. But these last few months of bachelor independence made him realize the restrictions which he had suffered earlier. Now there was no one to question his comings and goings. If he cared to stay out until two in the morning, there was no waiting tray, complete with hot chocolate in a vacuum flask, to reproach him. No parental note reminded him to bolt the door and switch off the landing light. It wasn't that he didn't love them, poor dear old things, thought Edward indulgently as he added more hot water to his bath, but simply that he had outgrown them.

'God bless Grandpa Howard!' said Edward aloud, as he sank back again.

It was good to be living in Caxley market square where his grandparents on both sides had built up their businesses. Here, in this house, of which he was now the proud owner, Bender North and his wife Hilda had lived for many years over their ironmongery shop. Edward could see his grandfather clearly now, in his mind's eye, a vast figure in a brown coat-overall striding among the coal scuttles and patty pans, the spades and milking pails, which jostled together beneath the pairs of hobnailed boots and hurricane lamps that swung from the ceiling above him. Soon afterwards, Bender and his wife had moved to Rose Lodge – a far more genteel address to Hilda's mind – and the glories of the great drawing room over the shop were no more. But Winnie, Edward's mother, and his Uncle Bertie North had described the red plush furniture, the plethora of ornaments and the floral arrangements of dried grasses and sea-lavender, with such vivid detail, that he felt quite familiar with the Edwardian splendour which had now vanished.

He knew, equally well, the sad story of the decline of Bender's business. It had been bought by a larger firm in the town and, later still, his grandfather Septimus Howard had taken it over. Sep still lived in the market square above his thriving bakery. The whole of the ground floor at North's he had transformed into a restaurant, almost ten years ago. It was, according to Caxley gossip, 'an absolute gold-mine', but there were few who grudged Sep Howard his success. Hardworking, modest, a pillar of the local chapel, and a councillor, the little baker's worth was appreciated by his fellow townsmen.

The business was to go to his son Robert, already a vigorous partner, when Sep could carry on no longer. Sep was now, in the early summer of 1939, a spry seventy-three, and there was no sign of his relinquishing his hold on family affairs. The acquisition of Bender's old home and the growth of the restaurant had given Sep an added interest in life. It was typical of his generosity, said his neighbours, that he had given Edward the house which had been Bender's when the boy attained the age of twenty-one. The restaurant, on the ground floor, would be Robert's in time, and the more shrewd of Caxley's citizens wondered why Sep could not foresee that there might be friction between Edward and his young uncle in the years to come.

But on this bright May morning all was well in Edward's world. It had needed courage to tell his two women-folk that he proposed to set up his own establishment, and even now, when he looked back on the scene at Rose Lodge, Edward winced.

15 The Market Square, still generally known in Caxley as 'North's', had fallen empty at Michaelmas 1938. The Parker family, who had been tenants for several years, had prospered, and bought a house in the village of Beech Green a few miles away. The property had become Edward's that same year on his twenty-first birthday. It was the most splendid present imaginable, for the boy had loved the house as long as he could remember. The idea of living there one day had been with him for many years, a secret joyous hope which he fully intended to turn into reality.

'It's a big responsibility for a young man in your position,' Grandma North quavered, when the old home was first made over to him. 'I know your Grandpa Howard has arranged for a sum of money to keep the place in repair, but what happens when he's gone? You may have a wife and family to keep by then.'

'We'll all live there,' cried Edward cheerfully, 'and you shall come and tell us how badly we keep it, compared with your days.'

'Well, you may laugh about it now, my boy,' said the old lady, a little querulously, 'but I know what a big place that is to keep going. The stairs alone are a morning's work, and no one ever managed to keep that back attic free from damp. Your Grandpa Howard's never lived there as I have. He's no notion of what it means in upkeep.'

Hilda North had never liked Septimus Howard. She had watched him rise as her own husband had steadily declined. Old age did not mellow her feelings towards this neighbour of a lifetime, and the marriage of her darling son Bertie to Kathy Howard and the earlier marriage of her daughter Winnie to Leslie, Edward's ne'er-do-well father, did nothing to allay the acrimony which she felt towards the Howard family.

'Thank God,' she said often to Edward, 'that you take after the North side of the family, despite your name. Your dear mother's been both father and mother to you. Really, I sometimes think it was a blessing your father left her. She's better without him.'

Edward was wise enough to keep a silent tongue when the old lady ran on in this vein. He knew quite well that there was a strong streak of the Howards in his make-up. He hoped, in all humility, that he had something of Sep Howard's strength of character. He was beginning to guess, with some astonishment, that he might possess some of his erring father's attraction for the opposite sex.

He often wondered about his father. It was impossible to get a clear picture of him from either side of the family, and his own memories were hazy. Leslie Howard had decamped with an earlier love when Edward was four and the second child, Joan, only a few months old. As far as was known, he flourished, as the wicked so often do, in a Devonshire town. He had never been seen in Caxley again.

'Too ashamed, let's hope!' said Edward's grandmother North tartly, but Edward sometimes wondered. What was the result of that flight from the family? He had never heard his father's side of the affair. It was as tantalizing as a tale half-read. Would he ever know the end of the story?

Edward had dropped the bombshell on a mellow September evening, a week or two before Michaelmas Day, when the Parkers were to vacate his newly acquired property. The two women were sitting in the evening sunshine admiring the brave show of scarlet dahlias. Around them, the gnats hummed. Above them, on the telephone wires, were ranged two or three dozen swallows like notes on staves of music. Soon they would be off to find stronger sunshine.

It was too bad to shatter such tranquillity, thought Edward, pacing restlessly about the garden, but it had to be done. He spoke as gently as his taut nerves allowed.

'Mother! Grandma!' He stopped before the two placid figures. Sun-steeped, vague and sleepy, they gazed at him with mild expectancy. Edward's heart smote him, but he took the plunge.

'Don't let this be too much of a shock, but I'm thinking about living in the market square myself when the Parkers leave.'

His mother's pretty mouth dropped open. His grandmother did not appear to have heard him. He raised his voice slightly.

'At the old house, Grandma dear. I want to move in at Michaelmas.'

'I heard you,' said the old lady shortly.

'But why, Edward? Why?' quavered his mother. 'Aren't you happy here?'

To Edward's alarm he saw tears welling in his mother's blue eyes. Just as he thought, there was going to be the devil of a scene. No help for it then, but to soldier on. He sat down on the iron arm of the curly garden seat upon which the two were reclining, and put a reassuring arm about his mother's shoulders.

'Of course I'm happy here –' he began.

'Then say no more,' broke in his mother swiftly. 'What should we do without a man in the house? We're so nicely settled, Edward, don't go upsetting things.'

'What's put this in your head?' queried his grandmother. 'Getting married, are you?'

'You know I'm not,' muttered Edward, rising from his perch and resuming his prowlings. 'It's simply that the house is now mine, it's empty, and I want to live there.'

'But it will be far too big for you alone, Edward,' protested his mother. 'And far too expensive.'

'I've worked it all out and I can manage quite well. I don't intend to use all the house, simply the top floor. The rest can be let, and bring me in a regular income.'

'Well, I must say,' cried his mother reproachfully, 'you seem to have been planning this move for some time! I can't tell you what a shock it is! I'd no idea you felt like this about things. What about poor Grandma? How do you think she is going to like it when there are only women left alone to cope with everything here?'

Winnie produced a handkerchief and mopped her eyes. Her mother, made of sterner stuff, sniffed militantly and Edward prepared to hear the old lady's vituperation in support of her daughter. What a hornet's nest he had disturbed, to be sure! But a surprise was in store.

'Let him go!' snapped old Mrs North testily. 'If he wants to go and ruin himself in that damp old shop by the river, then let him, silly young fool! I've lived alone before, and I won't be beholden to my grandchildren. He doesn't know when he's well off. Let him try managing that great place for a bit! He'll soon learn. And for pity's sake, Winnie, stop snivelling. Anyone'd think he was off to Australia the way you're carrying on!'

It had been too much to expect an ally at Rose Lodge, but the old lady's impatient dismissal of the affair greatly helped Edward. After a few uncomfortable days, whilst Edward tried to avoid his mother's martyred gaze and the sound of intermittent argument about the subject between the two women, he managed to make them see that he was adamant in his decision.

'Dash it all, I'm less than a mile away. I shall be in and out of Rose Lodge until you'll probably get fed up with me. I can do any odd jobs, and Tom comes twice a week for the garden. He's promised me to keep an eye on things. And you'll see Joan as regularly as you always do.'

Joan, Edward's sister, now eighteen, was in London, training to teach young children. Her vacations were lengthy and just occasionally she managed to get home on a Sunday during term-time. Edward had written to her telling of his plans and had received enthusiastic support. There was an unusually strong bond of affection between the brother and sister, forged in part by the absence of a father. Certainly, during the stormy period which preceded Edward's move, he was doubly grateful for Joan's encouragement.

As soon as the Parkers had gone to their new home, Edward put his plans into action. He decided to make the attic floor into his own domain, and the four rooms became a bedroom and sitting-room, both overlooking the market square and facing south, and a kitchen and bathroom at the back. He had papered and painted the rooms himself, and although the paper was askew in places and a suspicion of rust was already becoming apparent on the bathroom pipes, the whole effect was fresh and light.

Surveying his handiwork from the bath Edward felt a glow of pride. This was all his own. At times he could scarcely believe his good luck. The spacious rooms below were already occupied by a young bank clerk who had been at Caxley Grammar School with Edward some years before. He and his wife seemed careful tenants, likely to remain there for some time. Their first child was due in the autumn.

The future looked pretty bright, decided Edward, reviewing the situation. He enjoyed his work as an agricultural engineer at the county town some fifteen miles away, and promotion seemed likely before long. The family appeared to have come round completely to the idea of his living apart and no one could possibly realise how exciting he found his newly-won independence.

And then there was his flying. He had joined the R.A.F.V.R. when he was eighteen and had first flown solo on a bright spring day over two years ago. It was the culmination of an ambition which had grown steadily in fervour since he was ten. Now most weekends were spent at the aerodrome west of Caxley and his yearly holiday was earmarked for annual training. He liked the men he met there, their cheerful company and their predictable jokes, but better still he liked the machines with their fascinatingly complicated engines and their breathtakingly flimsy superstructure.

In a few hours he would be in the air again, he thought joyfully, looking down on the patchwork of brown and green fields far below. For this was one of the blessed Sundays when he set off early in his two-seater Morris in his carefully casual new sports jacket and a silk scarf knotted about his neck in place of the workaday tie.

He stood up in the bath and began to towel himself vigorously. A pigeon cooed on the gutter above the steamy window. Edward could see the curve of its grey breast against the sky.

'Two rashers and two eggs,' called Edward to the bird, above the gurgle of the bath water swirling down the waste pipe, 'and then I'm off!'

A thought struck him. The car's spare tyre was at Uncle Bertie's garage. He must remember to pick it up on his way. The possibility of a puncture somewhere on Salisbury Plain, even on a fine May morning such as this, was not to be borne, especially on a day dedicated to flying.

He shrugged himself into his shabby camel-hair dressing-gown and went, whistling, in search of the frying pan.

## THE SHADOW OF WAR

Edward's Uncle Bertie was his mother's brother and now the head of the North family. He lived in a four-square red-brick house some yards from the busy High Street of Caxley where his motor business flourished.

One approached Bertie's house by way of a narrow lane. It started as a paved alley between two fine old Georgian buildings which fronted the pavements, but gradually widened into a gravelled track which led eventually to the tow-path by the river Cax. Edward always enjoyed the sudden change from the noise of the street as he turned into this quiet backwater.

As he guessed, Bertie was already at work in the garden. Oil can in hand, he was bending over the mower when his nephew arrived. He straightened up and limped purposefully towards him, waving the oil can cheerfully. For a man who had lost one foot in the war, thought Edward, he moved with remarkable agility.

'You want your spare wheel,' said Bertie. 'I'll give you the garage key and you can help yourself.'

They moved towards the house, but Bertie

checked suddenly to point out a thriving rose which was growing against the wall.

'Look at that, my boy! I planted it when your Aunt Kathy and I married. Just look at the growth it's made in these few years!'

Edward looked obediently, but he was already impatient to be off to his flying. Catching sight of the expression on his handsome nephew's dark young face, Bertie threw back his head and laughed.

'You're no gardener, Edward! I forgot. Too bad to hold you up. Come and say "Hello" to the family before you set off.'

His Aunt Kathy was beating eggs in a big yellow basin. Her dark hair was tucked into a band round her head so that she looked as if she were wearing a coronet. How pretty she was, thought Edward, as slim and brown as a gipsy! No wonder Uncle Bertie had waited patiently for her all those years. He remembered Grandma North's tart comments to his mother on the marriage.

'I should've thought Bertie would have had more sense than to marry into the Howard family. Look what it brought you – nothing but unhappiness! And a widow too. Those two children will never take to a stepfather – even one as doting as dear Bertie. I can see nothing but misery ahead for that poor boy!'

' "That poor boy" ' is nearly forty,' his mother had replied with considerable vigour, 'and he's loved her all his life. Long faces and sharp tongues won't harm that marriage, you'll see.'

And all Caxley had seen. Bertie and Kathy, with her son and daughter by her first husband, were living proof of mature happiness, and when a son was born a year or so later, the little town rejoiced with them. Even Grandma North agreed grudgingly that it was all running along extraordinarily smoothly and put it down entirely to Bertie's exceptionally sweet North disposition.

'Where are the children?' asked Edward.

'Fishing,' replied Kathy, smiling. 'Unless you mean Andrew. He's asleep, I hope. He woke us at four this morning with train noises – shunting mostly. It makes an awful din.'

'That boy wants to look forward, not backwards,' observed Edward. 'He wants to get his mind on aeroplanes.'

'I think one air fanatic in the family is enough,' commented Bertie, handing over the key to the garage. 'Off you go. Have a good day.'

And Edward departed on the first stage of his journey westward.

'It would never surprise me,' said Bertie to his wife, when Edward had gone, 'to hear that Edward had decided to join the R.A.F. His heart's in aeroplanes, not tractors and binders.'

'But what about our business?' queried Kathy.

'I thought you'd planned for him to become a partner?'

'I shan't press the boy. We've two of our own to follow on if they want to.'

'But *flying*,' protested Kathy, sifting flour energetically into the beaten eggs. 'It's so dangerous, Bertie. Edward might be killed!'

'He might indeed,' observed Bertie soberly. And thousands more like him, he thought privately. He watched his pretty wife at her work, and thought, not for the first time, how much there was which he could not discuss with her. Did she ever, for one fleeting moment, face the fact that war was looming closer and closer? This uneasy peace which Chamberlain had procured at Munich could not last long. There was menace on every side. It must be met soon. Bertie knew in his bones that it was inevitable.

'What a long face!' laughed Kathy, suddenly looking up from her cooking. 'You look as though you'd lost a penny and found a halfpenny.'

She crossed the kitchen towards the oven, shooing him out of the way as if he were one of the children.

'It's time this sponge was in,' she cried. 'Don't forget Mum and Dad are coming to tea this afternoon. You'd better get on in the garden while the sun's out.'

She paused briefly by the window to gaze at the shining morning.

'Isn't it lovely, Bertie? When it's like this I can't believe it will ever be any different – just sunshine all the time. Do you feel that way too, Bertie?'

'I don't think I'm quite such an incurable optimist,' answered Bertie, lightly. 'More's the pity maybe.'

He made his way back to the mower, his thoughts still with him. The grass was still too wet to cut, he decided. He would take a stroll along the towpath and watch the river flowing gently eastward beneath the cloudless sky. There was something very comforting about flowing water when one's spirits were troubled.

He turned left outside his garden gate, his back to the town, and limped steadily towards the tunnel of green shade made by a dozen or so massive chestnut trees, now lit with hundreds of flower-candles, which lined the banks some quarter of a mile away. The sunshine was warm upon his back, and broke into a thousand fragments upon the surface of the running water, dazzling to the eye. Just before the dark cavern formed by the chestnut trees, the river was shallow, split by a long narrow island, the haven of moorhen and coot.

Here Bertie paused to rest his leg and to enjoy the sparkle of the fretted water and the rustling of the willow leaves on the islet. The shallows here were spangled with the white flowers of duckweed, their starry fragility all the more evident by contrast with a black dabchick who searched busily for food among them, undisturbed by Bertie's presence.

The mud at the side of the water glistened like brown satin and gave forth that peculiarly poignant river-smell which is never forgotten. A bee flew close to Bertie's ear and plopped down on the mud, edging its way to the brink of the water to drink. A water-vole, sunning itself nearby, took to the stream, and making for the safety of the island left an echelon of ripples behind its small furry head.

The change in temperature beneath the great chestnut trees was amazing. Here the air struck cold upon Bertie's damp forehead. The path was dark, the stones treacherously slimy and green with moss. There was something dark and secret about this part of the Cax. No wonder that the children loved to explore its banks at this spot! It was the perfect setting for adventure. To look back through the tunnel to the bright world which he had just traversed was an eerie experience. There it was all light, gaiety and warmth – a Kathy's world, he thought suddenly – where no terrors were permitted.

But here there was chill in the air, foreboding, and a sense of doom. He put a hand upon the rough bark of a massive trunk beside him and shuddered at its implacable coldness. Was this his world, at the moment, hostile, menacing, full of unaccountable fears?

He was getting fanciful, he told himself, retracing his steps. It was good to get back into the sunshine, among the darting birds and the shimmering insects which played above the kindly Cax. He would put his morbid thoughts behind him and return to the pleasures of the moment. There was the lawn to be cut and the dead daffodils to be tied up. He quickened his pace, advancing into the sunshine.

In the market square the bells of St Peter's called the citizens of Caxley to Matins. Under the approving eyes of the bronze Queen Victoria whose statue dominated the market place, a trickle of men, women and children made their way from the dazzling heat into the cool nave of the old church. The children looked back reluctantly as they mounted the steps. A whole hour of inaction, clad in white socks, tight Sunday clothes, and only the hat elastic wearing a pink groove under one's chin to provide entertainment and furtive nourishment, loomed ahead. What a wicked waste of fresh air and sunshine!

Septimus Howard and his wife Edna crossed the square from his bakery as the bells clamoured above them, but they were making their way to the chapel in the High Street where Sep and his forbears had worshipped regularly for many years.

Automatically, he glanced across at Howard's

Restaurant which occupied the entire ground floor beneath Edward's abode. The linen blinds were pulled down, the CLOSED card hung neatly in the door. His son Robert had done his work properly and left all ship-shape for the weekend. It was to be hoped, thought Sep, that he would be in chapel this morning. He was far too lax, in Sep's opinion, in his chapel-going. It set a poor example to the work people.

Edward's presence he could not hope to expect, for he and his sister Joan were church-goers, taking after the North side of the family. Not that they made many attendances, as Sep was well aware. He sympathized with Edward's passion for flying, but would have liked to see it indulged after he had done his duty to his Maker.

The congregation was sparse. No doubt many were gardening or had taken advantage of the warmth to drive with their families for a day at the sea. It was understandable, Sep mused, but indicative of the general slackening of discipline. Or was it perhaps an unconscious desire to snatch at happiness while it was still there? After the grim aftermath of the war, and the grimmer times of the early thirties, the present conditions seemed sweet. Who could blame people for living for the present?

Beside him Edna stirred on the hard seat. Her dark hair, scarcely touched with grey, despite her seventy years, curled against her cheek beneath a yellow straw hat nodding with silk roses and a golden haze of veiling. To Sep's eye it was really suitable headgear for the Sabbath, but it was impossible to curb Edna's exuberance when it came to clothes, and he readily admitted that it set off her undimmed beauty. He never ceased to wonder at the good fortune which had brought into his own quiet life this gay creature, whose presence gave him such comfort.

Now the minister was praying for peace in their time. Sep, remembering with infinite sadness the loss of his first-born Jim in the last war, prayed with fervent sincerity. What would happen to the Howards if war came again, as he feared it must? Robert, in his thirties, would go. Edward, no doubt, would be called up at once to the Royal Air Force. Leslie, his absent son whom he had not seen since he left Caxley and his wife Winnie years earlier, would be too old to be needed.

And he himself, at seventy-three? Thank God, he was still fit and active. He could continue to carry on his business and the restaurant too, and he would find time to work, as he had done earlier, for the Red Cross.

What dreadful thoughts for a bright May morning! Sep looked at the sunshine spilling lozenges of bright colour through the narrow windows across the floor of the chapel, and squared his shoulders.

He must trust in God. He was good and merciful. A way must surely be found for peace between nations. That man of wickedness, Adolf Hitler, would be put down in God's good time. He had reached the limit of his powers.

He followed Edna's nodding roses out into the sunny street. Someone passed with an armful of lilac, and its fragrance seemed the essence of early summer. Opposite, at the end of one of the roads leading to the Cax, he could see a magnificent copper beech tree, its young thin leaves making a haze of pink against the brilliant sky.

It was a wonderful day. It was a wonderful world. Surely, for men of faith, all would be well, thought Sep, retracing his steps to the market square.

But despite the warmth around him, there was a little chill in the old man's heart, as though the shadow of things to come had began to fall across a fine Sunday in May in the year 1939.

## EVACUEES IN CAXLEY

As the summer advanced, so did the menacing shadow of war. It was plain that Germany intended to subdue Poland, and Caxley people, in common with the rest of Britain, welcomed the Prime Minister's guarantee that Britain would stand by the threatened country. The memory of Czechoslovakia's fate still aroused shame.

'Hitler's for it if he tries that game again with

Poland,' said one worthy to another in the market square.

'If we gets the Russians on our side,' observed his crony, 'he don't stand a chance.'

There was a growing unity of purpose in the country. The ties with France, so vividly remembered by the older generation who had fought in the Great War, were being strengthened daily. If only the Government could come to favourable terms with Russia, then surely this tripartite alliance could settle Hitler's ambitions, and curb his alarming progress in Europe.

Meanwhile, plans went ahead for the evacuation of children, the issue of gas masks, the digging of shelters from air attacks, and all the civilian defence precautions which, if not particularly reassuring, kept people busy and certainly hardened their resolve to show Hitler that they meant business.

The three generations in the Howard and North families faced the threat of war typically. Septimus Howard, who had been in his fifties during the Great War of 1914–18, was sad but resolute.

'It's a relief,' he said, voicing the sentiments of all who heard him, 'to know where we stand, and to know that we are acting in the right way. That poor man Chamberlain has been sorely hoodwinked. He's not alone. There are mighty few people today who will believe that evil is still abroad and active. But now his eyes are opened, and he can see Hitler for what he is – a liar, and worse still, a madman.'

Bertie North, who had fought in France as a young man and had lost a foot as a result, knew that the war ahead would involve his family in Caxley as completely as it would engage the armed men. This, to him, was the real horror, and the thought of a gas attack, which seemed highly probable, filled him with fury and nausea. Part of him longed to send Kathy and the three children overseas to comparative safety, but he could not ignore that inward voice which told him that this would be the coward's way. Not that Kathy would go anyway – she had made that plain from the start. Where Bertie was, there the family would be, she maintained stoutly, and nothing would shake her.

Only two things gave Bertie any comfort in this dark time. First, he would return to the army, despite his one foot.

'Must be masses of paper work to do,' he told Sep. 'I can do that if they won't let me do anything more martial, and free another chap.'

The second thing was the attitude of mind, in which the young men most involved faced the situation. Bertie remembered with bitter pain the heroic dedication with which his own generation had entered the war. High ideals, noble sacrifices, chivalry, honour and patriotism had been the words – and not only the words – which sent a gallant and gay generation into battle. The awful aftermath had been doubly poignant.

Today there was as much courage and as much resolution. But the young men were not blinded by shining ideals. This would be a grim battle, probably a long one. There was no insouciant cry of 'Over by Christmas', as there had been in 1914. They were of a generation which knew that it was fighting for survival, and one which knew too that in modern warfare there is no real victor. Whatever the outcome it would be a long road to recovery when the war itself was past.

Nevertheless, for Edward and his friends, hearts beat a little faster as action appeared imminent. What if Hitler had annexed an alarming amount of Europe? The Low Countries and France would resist to a man, and the English Channel presented almost as great an obstacle to an invader today as it did to Napoleon. This year had given England time to get ahead with preparations. The uneasy peace, bought by Mr Chamberlain at Munich a year earlier, may have been a bad thing, but at least it had provided a breathing space.

'Thank God I'm trained for something!' cried Edward to his mother. 'Think of all those poor devils who will be shunted into the army and sent foot-slogging all over Europe! At least I shall have some idea of what I'm to do.'

He spent as much time training now as he could possibly manage. He had a purpose. It was a sober one, but it gave him inward courage. Whatever happened, he intended to be as ready and fit as youth, good health and steady application to his flying would allow.

Edward, most certainly, was the happiest man in the family despite the fact that he was the most vulnerable.

During the last week of August it became known that all hope of an alliance with Russia had gone. Triumphantly the Nazis announced a pact with the Soviet Union. Things looked black indeed for England and her allies, but assurances went out again. Whatever happened, Britain would stand by her obligations to Poland. After a period of anxiety over Russia's negotiations, it was good to know the truth.

On 24 August the Emergency Powers Bill was passed, together with various formalities for calling up the armed forces. Edward's spirits rose when he heard the news at six o'clock. How soon, he wondered, before he set off?

It was a few days later that the House of Commons met again. The question facing the country, said one speaker, was: 'Shall one man or one country be allowed to dominate Europe?' To that question there could be only one answer.

People in Caxley now prepared to receive evacuees from London and another nearby vulnerable town into their midst. No one could pretend that this move was wholeheartedly welcome. The genuine desire to help people in danger and to afford them a port in a storm, was tempered with doubts. Would strangers fit into the home? Would they be content? Would they be cooperative?

Sep and Edna had offered to take in six boys of school age. If they could have squeezed in more they would have done. Frankly, Edna welcomed the idea of children in the house again. The thought that they might be unruly, disobedient or difficult to handle, simply did not enter her head or Sep's.

'It is the least we can do,' said Sep gravely. 'How should we feel if we had ever had to send our children to strangers?'

Bertie and Kathy expected a mother and baby to be billeted with them in the house by the river. The fate of Edward's flat was undecided at the moment, and the future of Rose Lodge hung in the balance. There was talk of its being requisitioned as a nurses' hostel, in which case Winnie and her mother might move back to Edward's new domain in the market square.

'Proper ol' muddle, ennit?' observed the dustman to Edward. 'Still, we've got to show that Hitler.' He sighed gustily.

'Wicked ol' rat,' continued the dustman, 'getting 'is planes filled up with gas bombs, no doubt. You see, that's what'll 'appen first go off. You wants to keep your gas mask 'andy as soon as the balloon goes up. Can't think what them Germans were playing at ever to vote 'im in.'

He replaced the dustbin lid with a resounding clang.

'Ah, well,' he said indulgently, 'they're easy taken in – foreigners!'

And with true British superiority he mounted the rear step of the dust lorry and rode away.

It was on Friday, 1 September that evacuation began and Caxley prepared for the invasion. Beds were aired, toys brought down from attics, welcoming nosegays lodged on bedroom mantelpieces and pies and cakes baked for the doubtless starving visitors.

'Isn't it odd,' remarked Joan Howard to her mother, as she staggered from the doorstep with a double supply of milk, 'how we expect evacuees to be extra cold and extra hungry? We've put twice as many blankets on their beds as ours, and we've got in enough food to feed an army.'

'I know,' agreed Winnie. 'It's on a par with woollies and shoes. Have you noticed how everyone is buying one or two stout pairs of walking shoes and knitting thick sweaters like mad? I suppose we subconsciously think we'll be marching away westward when war comes, with only a good thick sweater to keep out the cold when we're asleep under a hedge at night.'

'Very sensible,' approved old Mrs North, who was busy repairing a dilapidated golliwog which had once been Joan's. 'I can't think why you don't take my advice and stock up with Chilprufe underclothes. You'll regret it this time next year. Why I remember asking Grandpa North for five pounds when war broke out in 1914, and I laid it out on vests, combinations, stockings, tea towels and pillow slips – and never ceased to be thankful!'

Joan laughed. Despite the horrors which must surely lie ahead, life was very good at the moment. She had just obtained a teaching post at an infants' school in the town and was glad to be living at home to keep an eye on her mother and grandmother. As soon as things were more settled, however, she secretly hoped to join the W.A.A.F. or the A.T.S. Who knows? She might be posted somewhere near Edward.

It was not yet known if Rose Lodge would be wanted to house an influx of nurses. Meanwhile, the three women had prepared two bedrooms for their evacuees.

Winnie and Joan left the house in charge of old Mrs North and made their way towards the station. The local Reception Officer was in charge there, assisted by a dozen or so local teachers. Winnie and her daughter were bound for a school which stood nearby. Here the children would come with their teachers to collect their rations for forty-eight hours and to rest before setting off for their new homes. Winnie was attached to the Women's Voluntary Service Corps and as Joan's school was closed for the time being she had offered to go and help.

A train had just arrived at the station, and the children were being marshalled into some semblance of order by harassed teachers. The children looked pathetic, Joan thought, clutching bundles and cases, and each wearing a label. A gas mask, in a neat cardboard box, bounced on every back or front, and one's first impression was of a band of refugees, pale and shabby.

But, on looking more closely, Joan noticed the cheeks which bulged with sweets, the occasional smile which lightened a tired face and the efficient mothering by little girls of children smaller than themselves. Given a good night's rest, Joan decided, these young ones would turn out to be as cheerful and resilient a lot as she had ever met during her training in London.

Inside the school hall an army of helpers coped with earlier arrivals. To Joan's secret delight, and her mother's obvious consternation, she saw that Miss Mobbs was in charge. This formidable individual had once been a hospital sister in the Midlands but retired to Caxley to look after a bachelor brother some years before.

'Poor man,' Caxley said. 'Heaven knows what he's done to deserve it! There's no peace now for him.'

But running a home and cowing a brother were not enough for Miss Mobbs. Within a few weeks she was a driving force in several local organisations, and the scourge of those who preferred a quiet life.

At the moment she was in her element. Clad in nurse's costume, her fourteen-stone figure dominated the room as she swept from table to table and queue to queue, rallying her forces.

'That's the way, kiddies,' she boomed. 'Hurry along. Put your tins in your carrier bags and don't keep the ladies waiting!'

'Old boss-pot,' muttered one eight-year-old to her companion, much to Joan's joy. ' 'Ope 'Itler gets 'er.'

Miss Mobbs bore down upon Winnie.

'We've been looking for you, Mrs Howard. This way. A tin of meat for every child and your daughter can do the packets of sugar.'

Joan observed, with mingled annoyance and amusement, that her mother looked as flustered and apologetic as any little probationer nurse and then remembered that, of course, years ago her mother really had been one. Obviously the voice of authority still twanged long-silent chords.

'Better late than never,' remarked Miss Mobbs with false heartiness. But her strongly disapproving countenance made it quite apparent that the Howards were in disgrace.

Glasses flashing, she sailed briskly across the room to chivvy two exhausted teachers into line, leaving Joan wondering how many more women were adding thus odiously to the horrors of warfare.

She and her mother worked steadily from ten

until four, handing out rations to schoolchildren and their teachers and to mothers with babies. A brief lull midday enabled them to sip a cup of very unpleasant coffee and to eat a thinly spread fishpaste sandwich. Joan, whose youthful appetite was lusty, thought wistfully of the toothsome little chicken casserole her mother had left in the oven for Grandma North, and was unwise enough to mention it in Miss Mobbs' hearing.

'It won't hurt some of us to tighten our belts,' claimed that redoubtable lady, clapping a large hand over her own stiff leather one. Joan noticed, uncharitably, that it was fastened at the last hole already.

'We shan't beat Hitler without a few sacrifices,' she continued, putting three spoonsful of sugar into her coffee, 'and we must be glad of this chance of doing our bit.'

Really, thought Joan, speechless with nausea, it was surprising that Miss Mobbs had not been lynched, and could only suppose that the preoccupation of those present, and perhaps a more tolerant attitude towards this ghastly specimen than her own, accounted for Miss Mobbs' preservation.

At four o'clock they returned to Rose Lodge to find that their own evacuees had arrived and were already unpacking. Two women teachers, one a middle-aged widow, and the other a girl not much older than Joan, were sharing Edward's former room, and a young mother with a toddler and a six-week-old baby occupied the larger bedroom at the back of the house which had been Joan's until recently.

Grandmother North, trim and neat, her silver hair carefully waved and her gold locket pinned upon her dark silk blouse, was preparing tea. She looked as serene and competent as if she were entertaining one or two of her old Caxley friends. Only the flush upon her cheeks gave any hint of her excitement at this invasion.

'Where are we having it?' asked Joan, lifting the tray.

'In the drawing-room, of course,' responded her grandmother. 'Where else?'

'I thought – with so many of us,' faltered Joan, 'that we might have it here, or set it in the dining-room.'

'Just because we're about to go to war,' said Grandma North with hauteur, 'it doesn't follow that we have to lower our standards.'

She poured boiling water into the silver tea pot, and Joan could not help remembering the advertisement which she had read in *The Caxley Chronicle* that morning. Side by side with injunctions to do without, and to tackle one's own repairs in order to leave men free for war work, was the usual story from a local employment agency.

'Patronized by the Nobility and Gentry,' ran the heading, followed by:

'Titled lady requires reliable butler and housekeeper. 4 in family. 3 resident staff.'

There was a touch of this divine lunacy about her grandmother, thought Joan with amusement, and gave her a quick peck of appreciation.

'Mind my hair, dear,' said Mrs North automatically, and picking up the teapot she advanced to meet her guests.

'We're going to be a pretty rum household,' was Joan's private and unspoken comment as she surveyed the party when they were gathered together. Grandma North sat very upright behind the tea tray. Her mother, plump and kindly, carried food to the visitors, while she herself did her best to put the young mother at her ease and to cope with Bobby's insatiable demands for attention. This fat two-year-old was going to cause more damage at Rose Lodge than the rest of them put together, Joan surmised.

Already he had wiped a wet chocolate biscuit along the cream chintz of the armchair, and tipped a generous dollop of milk into his mother's lap, his own shoes and Joan's. Now he was busy hammering bread and butter into the carpet with a small, greasy and powerful fist. His mother made pathetic and ineffectual attempts to control him.

'Oh, you are a naughty boy, Bobby! Look at the lady's floor! Give over now!'

'Please don't worry,' said Grandma North, a shade frostily. 'We can easily clean it up later.'

Joan felt sorry for the young mother. Exhausted with travelling, parted from a husband who had rejoined his ship the day before, and wholly overwhelmed by all that had befallen her, she seemed near to tears. As soon as was decently possible, she hurried Bobby upstairs to bed and made her escape.

Mrs Forbes, the older teacher, seemed a sensible pleasant person, though from the glint in her eye as she surveyed Bobby's tea-time activities, it was plain that she would have made use of a sharp slap or two to restrain that young gentleman. Her companion, Maisie Hunter, was a fresh-faced curly-haired individual whose appetite, Joan noticed, was as healthy as her own.

How would they all shake down together, she wondered, six women, and two babies – well, one baby and a two-year-old fiend might be a more precise definition – under the roof of Rose Lodge? Time alone would tell.

## WAR BREAKS OUT

By Sunday morning, the visitors at Rose Lodge appeared to have settled down. This was by no means general in Caxley. Already, much to the billeting authorities' dismay, some mothers and children were making their way back to the danger zone in preference to the dullness of country living. Others were making plans to be fetched back to civilization during the week. Their hosts were torn between relief and the guilty feeling that they had failed in their allotted task of welcoming those in need.

The early news on the wireless said that the Prime Minister would speak at eleven-fifteen, and Mrs North invited the household to assemble in the drawing-room.

'I suppose this is it,' said Joan.

'And about time too,' rapped out the old lady. 'All this shilly-shallying!'

She, with Winnie and Joan were going to lunch at Bertie's. The parents of the young mother, Nora Baker, were coming to spend the day, and Mrs Forbes' son was paying a last visit before setting off to an army camp in the north.

'Let them have the house to themselves for the day,' Bertie said, 'and come and see us.'

And so it had been arranged.

Just before the broadcast, the inhabitants of Rose Lodge settled themselves in the drawing-room. Bobby, mercifully, had been put into his cot for his morning sleep, but the baby, freshly-bathed and fed, kicked happily on the floor enjoying the admiration of so many women.

By now it was known that an ultimatum had been handed to Germany to expire at 11 a.m. There was a feeling of awful solemnity when finally the Prime Minister's voice echoed through the room. There had been no reply to the ultimatum, he told his anxious listeners, and in consequence we were already at war.

Joan felt a cold shiver run down her back. She shot a glance at the older women around her. Their faces were grave and intent. Only Nora Baker and her baby seemed unaffected by the terrible words. The baby gazed with blue, unfocused eyes at the ceiling, and its mother nodded and smiled gently.

'It is the evil things we shall be fighting against,' said Mr Chamberlain, 'brute force, bad faith, injustice, oppression and persecution.'

Old Mrs North nodded emphatically. A little nerve twitched at the corner of her mouth, but otherwise she looked calm and approving.

The speech ended and she turned off the set.

'Thank goodness, that poor man has done the right thing at last,' she said.

'Well, we know where we are,' agreed Mrs Forbes.

She had hardly finished speaking when the sound of wailing came from the distance, to be followed, seconds later, with a similar sound, five times as loud, as the air-raid siren at the Fire Station sent out its spine-chilling alarm.

'It *can't* be an air raid,' whispered Winnie. They all gazed at each other in incredulous perplexity.

'Trust the Germans,' said Mrs Norah brisky.

'Too efficient by half. And where did I leave my gas mask?'

'Gas!' gasped little Mrs Baker, snatching up the baby. She had become a greenish colour, and the child's pink face close to hers made her appear more terror-stricken than ever.

'I'll go and get the gas masks,' said Joan, and began methodically to shut the windows. How idiotic and unreal it all seemed, she thought, suddenly calm.

'I must get Bobby,' cried the young mother. 'Oh, my Gawd, who'd think we'd get gassed so soon?'

'I'll fetch him,' said Winnie. She and Joan ran upstairs to collect their gas masks, a bottle of brandy and – no one quite knew why – a rug and a box of barley sugar. Meanwhile the two teachers ran around the house closing windows and looking anxiously up into the sky for enemy invaders.

They were hardly back in the drawing-room before the sirens sounded again, but this time on one long sustained note which, they were to learn, heralded safety.

'That's the "All Clear",' cried Joan. 'What can have happened?'

'Very confusing,' said her grandmother severely. 'It was far better arranged in our war, with the Boy Scouts blowing bugles.'

'No doubt someone pressed the wrong button,' said Winnie. 'What a fright to give us all!'

Mrs Baker, her baby clutched to her bosom and a very disgruntled and sleepy Bobby clinging to her skirt, had tears running down her face. The others did their best to comfort her, and Joan insisted on administering a dose of brandy. It seemed a pity to have brought it all the way downstairs, she thought, and to take it back again unopened.

'D'you think it's safe to put them upstairs to sleep?' asked Mrs Baker pathetically.

'Perfectly,' said old Mrs North. 'Take my word for it, that stupid fellow Taggerty's at the bottom of this. Fancy putting him in charge at the A.R.P. place! If he's anything like that foolish cousin of his we had in the shop, he'll lose his head on every possible occasion. I hope he gets thoroughly reprimanded.'

'I don't think Taggerty has anything to do with it,' began Winnie. But her mother was already across the hall and beginning to mount the stairs.

'We must hurry,' she was saying. 'Bertie asked us there for twelve and we mustn't keep the dear boy waiting.'

If they had just ejected a troublesome wasp from the drawing-room she could not have been less concerned, thought Joan in admiration, following her small, upright figure aloft.

To Joan's and Winnie's delight, Edward was at Bertie's.

'We tried to ring you last night,' cried his

mother, 'but there was no reply. How did you get on?'

'Don't talk about it,' said Edward, throwing up his hands despairingly. 'I trotted along to report at the town centre and I'm on *indefinite leave*, if you please! *Indefinite leave!*'

'What exactly does that mean, dear?' asked Winnie anxiously.

'It means that I go back to work as usual, and sit on my bum waiting to be called up.'

'Language, Edward, language!' interjected his grandmother severely. 'There's no need to be vulgar just because you're disappointed.'

'No uniform?' said Joan.

'Only when I report each week,' said Edward. 'It seems the training units are bunged up at present. I suppose our turn'll come, but it's the hell of a nuisance, this hanging about.'

'At least you know what you will be doing when you do get started,' comforted Bertie. 'How are your evacuees, Mamma?'

'Very pleasant people,' said the old lady firmly. 'And yours?'

'Gone home,' said Kathy entering. 'Took one look at the bedroom and said it wasn't what they were used to.'

'Now, I wonder how you take that?' queried Joan.

'With a sigh of relief,' said Bertie, taking up the carving knife. 'She was quite the ugliest woman I've ever clapped eyes on, and the babies were something fearful. Enough to give us all night terrors.'

'Now, Bertie!' said his mother reprovingly. 'Don't exaggerate!'

'The trouble is,' said Edward, looking at his Aunt Kathy, 'your standards are too high. You don't know when you're well off.'

Bertie made no reply. But he smiled as he tackled the joint.

During the next few weeks, Caxley folk and their visitors did their best to shake down together, while the seasonal work went on in the mellow September sunshine. The harvest was gathered in, corn stacked, apples picked. In the kitchens frugal housewives made stores of jam and preserves, bottled their fruit and tomatoes and put eggs to keep in great buckets of isinglass.

Those who remembered the food shortages of the earlier war told gruesome tales to younger women.

'And I had to feed my family on puddings made of chicken maize on more than one occasion,' said one elderly evacuee. 'And not a spoonful of sugar to be had. You stock up with all you can. Rationing'll be tighter still this time.'

There was general dismay among farmers who had lost land to the defence departments. 'Where corn used to grow for hundreds of years,' *The Caxley Chronicle* reported one as saying, 'camps are now sprouting in profusion. Thousands of acres of good farmland have been sterilized for artillery ranges, exercise grounds for tanks, barracks and aerodromes.'

Edward, reading this at his solitary breakfast table snorted impatiently. They'd got to train *somewhere*, hadn't they? Oh, if only he could get started!

He flipped over the page.

'Petrol rationing hits delivery vans,' he read. 'Old cycles being brought out again.'

His eye caught a more bizarre morsel of wartime news.

'New Forest ponies may be painted with white stripes to make them more visible to motorists in the black-out.'

Edward laughed aloud.

'Good old *Caxley Chronicle!* And what's on at the flicks this week?'

Will Hay in *Ask a Policeman* and Jessie Matthews in *Climbing High*, he read with approval. Below the announcement was a new wartime column headed 'Your Garden and Allotment in Wartime.'

'Thank God I'm spared that,' exclaimed Edward, throwing the paper into a chair. But the caption had reminded him that he had promised his Uncle Robert, who so lovingly tended the garden of their shared premises, that he would give him a lift this morning on his way to work.

Edward's Uncle Robert was the youngest of Sep

Howard's children and only eleven years older than Edward. He felt towards this youthful uncle rather as he did towards the youngest child of Bender and Hilda North, his attractive aunt Mary, who was much the same age as Robert. They seemed more like an older brother and sister than members of an earlier generation.

Aunt Mary he saw seldom these days, which was a pity. She was a moderately successful actress, better endowed with dazzling good looks than brain, but hard working and with the good health and even temper which all three North children enjoyed.

'A messy sort of life,' Grandpa Sep Howard had commented once. 'I'm glad no child of mine wanted to take it up.' To Sep, staunch chapel-goer, there was still something of the scarlet woman about an actress.

Robert, of course, Edward saw almost daily. He did part of the supervision of Howard's bakery at the corner of the market square, but spent the major part of his time in running the restaurant on the ground floor below Edward's establishment.

Howard's Restaurant had flourished from the first and had now been in existence for about eight years. Sep's dream of little white tables and chairs set out on the lawn at the back of the property had come true. The garden, which had been Bender North's joy, remained as trim and gay as ever and added considerably to Caxley's attractions in the summer.

'I suppose you won't be running this little bus much longer,' observed Robert as they sped along.

'I've just enough petrol to keep her going for about a fortnight. With any luck I'll be posted by then.'

Robert was silent. Edward would dearly have liked to know Robert's feelings about the war, but he did not like to ask. No doubt Robert's job would be considered as a highly necessary one and he would be more advantageously employed there than in some humdrum post in one of the services. Nevertheless, Edward had not heard him mention volunteering or offering his services in any more martial capacity, despite the fact that he was only in his early thirties. In some ways, Edward mused, Robert was a rum fish.

Take this stupid business of his tenants, the couple who lived below his own flat and above Robert's restaurant, thought Edward. They were quiet people, taking care to be unobtrusive, but Robert had complained bitterly to Edward that the ceiling of the café was flaking and that this was due to the 'banging about upstairs.'

'And they had the cheek to say that the cooking smells from my restaurant went up into their sitting-room,' asserted Robert.

'Daresay they do, too,' said Edward equably.

'There's a pretty high stink of frying sometimes. I can even get a whiff on the floor above them.'

Robert's face had darkened.

'Well, you knew what to expect when you came to live over a restaurant,' he said shortly. 'The old man was a fool ever to think the property could be divided. The floors above my bit should have been kept for storing things.'

Edward had been amazed at the depth of feeling with which Robert spoke. For the first time in his carefree life, Edward realised that he was encountering jealousy, and a very unpleasant sight it was. Luckily, he had inherited a goodly portion of the Norths' equanimity and could reply evenly. But the barb stuck, nevertheless.

He dropped Robert now at his wholesaler's and drove on to the office. If only his posting would come through! There was no interest in his work during these tedious waiting days, and he was getting thoroughly tired of Caxley too, as it was at present. He was fed up with hearing petty tales about evacuees' head-lice and wet beds; and fed up too with the pomposity of some of the Caxleyites in positions of wartime authority. Somehow, in these last few weeks Caxley had become insupportable. He felt like a caged bird, frantic to try his wings, in more ways than one.

Ah well, sighed Edward philosophically as he turned into the yard at the side of the office, it couldn't be long now. Meanwhile, Will Hay and

Jessie Matthews were on at the flicks. He would ask that nice little teacher, Maisie Something-or-other at Rose Lodge, to accompany him. At least it was a new face in dull old Caxley.

Edward was not alone in his frustration. This was the beginning of a period which later became known as 'the phoney war', when the Allied forces and those of the Germans faced each other in their fortresses and nothing seemed to happen.

*The Caxley Chronicle* echoed the general unease. 'Don't eat these berries!' said one heading. Foster parents should make sure that their charges knew what deadly nightshade looked like. Could they distinguish between mushrooms and toadstools?

The Post Office issued a tart announcement pointing out that it had a much depleted staff and far more work than usual.

Someone wrote to say that country people were being exploited. Why should a farm labourer, with about thirty shillings a week left after paying his insurance, feed the parents of his two evacuees when they spent Sundays with them? And who was expected to pay for the new mattress that was needed? There was no doubt about it – the heroic spirit in which the nation had faced the outbreak of war was fast evaporating, in this anti-climax of domestic chaos and interminable waiting.

'If anyone else tells me to Stand By or to

Remain Alert,' said Bertie dangerously, 'I shall not answer for the consequences.'

'It's better than being told We're All In It Together,' consoled Kathy.

Joan, meanwhile, had started her new job, for the schools had reopened. A London school's nursery unit had been attached to the combined infants' school and this was housed in the Friends' Meeting House, a pleasant red-brick building perched on a little grassy knoll on the northern outskirts of Caxley. A Viennese teacher, who had escaped a few months before Austria was overrun by the Nazis, was in charge, and Joan was her willing assistant.

She loved the chattering children in their blue and white checked overalls. The day seemed one mad rush from crisis to crisis. There was milk to be administered, potties to empty, dozens of small hands and faces to wash, tears to be quenched, passions to be calmed and a hundred activities to take part in.

She loved, too, the atmosphere of the old premises. It was an agreeably proportioned building with high arched windows along each side. Round the walls were dozens of large wooden hat pegs used by Quakers of past generations. The floor was of scrubbed boards, charming to look at but dangerously splintery for young hands and knees.

Outside was a grassy plot. In one half stood a dozen or so small headstones over the graves of good men and women now departed. There was something very engaging, Joan thought, to see the babies tumbling about on the grass, and supporting themselves by the little headstones. Here the living and the dead met companionably in the autumn sunlight, and the war seemed very far away indeed.

A steep flight of stone steps led from the road to the top of the grassy mound upon which the Meeting House stood. An old iron lamp, on an arched bracket, hung above the steps, and Joan often thought what a pleasant picture the children made as they swarmed up the steps beneath its graceful curve, clad in their blue and white.

Her mother came on two afternoons a week to help with the children. Three afternoons were spent at the hospital, for Winnie did not want to tie herself to a regular full-time job, but preferred to do voluntary service when and where she could. There was her mother to consider and the evacuees. Winnie determined to keep Rose Lodge running as smoothly as she could, and only prayed that the proposal that it should be turned into a nurses' hostel would be quietly forgotten.

She found the small children amusing but thoroughly exhausting. The nursing afternoons were far less wearing.

She said as much to Joan as they walked home together one afternoon, scuffling the fallen leaves which were beginning to dapple the footpath with red and gold.

'I suppose it's because I was trained to nurse,' she remarked.

'Rather you than me,' responded Joan. 'It's bad enough mopping up a grazed knee. Anything worse would floor me completely.'

They turned into the drive of Rose Lodge and saw old Mrs North at the open front door. She was smiling.

'You've just missed Edward on the telephone. He's as pleased as a dog with two tails. He's posted at last to – now, what was it? – a flying training school in Gloucestershire.'

'Well,' said Joan thankfully, 'there's one happy fellow in Caxley tonight!'

## GRIM NEWS

Edward arrived at the flying training school on a dispiritingly bleak October afternoon. The aerodrome lay on a windswept upland, not unlike his own downland country. In the distance, against the pewter-grey sky, a line of woods appeared like a navy-blue smudge on the horizon; but for mile upon mile the broad fields spread on every side, some a faded green, some ashen with bleached stubble and some newly-furrowed with recent ploughing.

Edward surveyed the landscape from a window by his bed. His sleeping quarters were grimly austere. A long army hut, with about ten iron beds on each side, was now his bedroom. A locker stood by each bed, and the grey blankets which served as coverlets did nothing to enliven the general gloom.

But at any rate, thought Edward hopefully, he had a window by his allotted place and the hut was warm.

There was an old man working some twenty yards from the window where a shallow ditch skirted a corner of the aerodrome. A row of pollarded willows marked the line of the waterway, and the old man was engaged in slashing back the long straight boughs. His coat was grey and faded in patches, his face lined and thin. He wore no hat, and as he lunged with the bill-hook, his sparse grey hair rose and fell in the wind. It reminded Edward of the grey wool which catches on barbed wire, fluttering night and day throughout the changing seasons.

He seemed to be part of the bleached and colourless background – as gnarled and knotty as the willow boles among which he worked, as dry and wispy as the dead grass which rustled against his muddy rubber boots. But there was an intensity of purpose in his rhythmic slashing which reminded Edward, with a sudden pang, of his grandfather Sep Howard, so far away.

He turned abruptly from the window, straightened his tunic, and set off through the wind to the sergeants' mess.

He entered a large room furnished with plenty of small tables, armchairs, magazines and a bar. The aerodrome was one of the many built during the thirties, and still had, at the outbreak of war, its initial spruceness and comfort.

Edward fetched himself some tea, bought some cigarettes, and made his way towards a chair strategically placed by a bronze radiator. He intended to start the crossword puzzle in the newspaper which was tucked securely under his elbow. There were only five or six other men in the mess, none of whom he knew. But he had scarcely drunk half his tea and pencilled in three words of the puzzle before he was accosted by a newcomer.

'So you're here too?' cried his fellow sergeant pilot. Edward's heart sank.

There was nothing, he supposed, violently wrong with Dickie Bridges, but he was such a confoundedly noisy ass. He had met him first during voluntary training and found him pleasant enough company on his own, but unbearably boastful and excitable when a few of his contemporaries appeared. When parties began to get out of hand you could bet your boots that Dickie Bridges would be among the first to sling a glass across the room with a carefree whoop. He was, in peacetime, an articled clerk with a firm of solicitors in Edward's county town.

Rumour had it that their office was dark and musty, the partners, who still wore wing collars and cravats, were approaching eighty, one was almost blind and the other deaf. However, as they saw their clients together, one was able to hear them and the other to see them, and the office continued to function in a delightfully Dickensian muddle. Edward could only suppose that with such a restricting background it was natural that Dickie should effervesce when he escaped.

Edward made welcoming noises and made room on the table for Dickie's tea cup. Typical of life, he commented to himself, that of all the chaps he knew in the Volunteer Reserve, it should be old Dickie who turned up! Nevertheless, it was good to see a familiar face in these strange surroundings and he settled back to hear the news.

'Know this part of the world?' asked Dickie, tapping one of Edward's cigarettes on the table top.

'No. First time here.'

'Couple of decent little pubs within three miles,' Dickie assured him. 'But twenty-odd miles to any bright lights – not that we'll see much of those with the blackout, and I hear we're kept down to it pretty well here.'

'Better than kicking about at home,' said Edward. 'I would have been round the bend in another fortnight.'

'Me too,' agreed Dickie.

Edward remembered the two old partners in Dickie's professional life and inquired after them.

'They've both offered their military services,' chuckled Dickie, 'but have been asked to stand by for a bit. If they can't get into the front line they have hopes of being able to man a barrage balloon in the local park. Even the blind one says he can see *that!*'

Edward, amused, suddenly felt a lift of spirits. Could Hitler ever hope to win against such delicious and lunatic determination? He found himself warming towards Dickie, and agreeing to try one of the two decent little pubs the next evening.

Back at Caxley the winter winds were beginning to whistle about the market square, and people were looking forward to their first wartime Christmas with some misgiving. The news was not good. A number of merchant ships had been sunk and it was clear that Hitler intended to try to cut the nation's lifelines with his U-boats.

Cruisers, battleships and destroyers had all been recent casualties, and there seemed to be no more encouraging news from the B.E.F. in France.

The evacuees were flocking back to their homes and the people of Caxley folded sheets and took down beds wondering the while how soon they would be needed again. Petrol rationing, food rationing and the vexatious blackout aggravated the misery of 'the phoney war'. In particular, men like Bertie, who had served in the First World War and were anxious to serve in the present conflict, could get no satisfaction about their future plans.

Sep Howard had added worries. His supplies were cut down drastically, and some of his finest ingredients, such as preserved fruit and nuts, were now impossible to obtain. It grieved Sep to use inferior material, but it was plain that there was no alternative. 'Quality', or 'carriage trade', as he still thought of it, had virtually gone, although basic fare such as bread and buns had increased in volume because of the evacuees in Caxley. His workers were reduced in numbers, and petrol rationing severely hampered deliveries.

But business worries were not all. His wife Edna was far from well and refused to see a doctor. Since the outbreak of war she had served in the shop, looked after the six evacuee boys, and run her home with practically no help. She attacked everything with gay gusto and made light of the giddiness which attacked her more and more frequently.

' 'Tis nothing,' she assured the anxious Sep. 'Indigestion probably. Nothing that a cup of herb tea won't cure.'

The very suggestion of a doctor's visit put her into a panic.

'He'll have me in hospital in two shakes, and I'd die there! Don't you dare fetch a doctor to me, Sep.'

It was as though, with advancing age, she was returning to the gipsy suspicions and distrust of her forbears. She had always loved to be outside, and now, even on the coldest night, would lie beneath a wide-open window with the wind blowing in upon her. Sep could do nothing with the wilful woman whom he adored, but watch over her with growing anxiety.

One Sunday evening they returned from chapel as the full moon rose. In the darkened town its silvery light was more welcome than ever, and Edna stopped to gaze at its beauty behind the pattern of interlaced branches. She was like a child still, thought Sep, watching her wide dark eyes.

'It makes me feel excited,' whispered Edna. 'It always has done, ever since I was little.'

She put her hand through Sep's arm and they paced homeward companionably, Edna's eyes upon the moon.

It was so bright that night that Sep was unable to sleep. Beside him Edna's dark hair stirred in the breeze from the window. Her breathing was light and even. A finger of moonlight glimmered on the brass handles of the oak chest of drawers which had stood in the same position for all their married life. Upon it stood their wedding photograph, Edna small and enchantingly gay, Sep pale and very solemn. The glass gleamed in the silvery light.

It was very quiet. Only the bare branches stirred outside the window, and very faintly, with an ear long attuned to its murmur, Sep could distinguish the distant rippling of the Cax.

An owl screeched and at that moment Edna awoke. She sat up, looking like a startled child in her white nightgown, and began to cough. Sep raised himself.

'It hurts,' she gasped, turning towards him, her face puckered with astonishment. Sep put his arms round her thin shoulders. She seemed as light-boned as a bird.

She turned her head to look at the great glowing face of the moon shining full and strong at the open window. Sighing, she fell softly back against Sep's shoulder, her cloud of dark hair brushing his mouth. A shudder shook her body and her breath escaped with a queer bubbling sound.

In the cold moonlit silence of the bedroom, Sep knew with awful certainty that he held in his arms the dead body of his wife.

In the months that followed Sep drifted about his affairs like a small pale ghost. He attended to the shop, the restaurant, his chapel matters and council affairs with the same grave courtesy which was customary, but the spirit seemed to have gone from him, and people told each other that Sep had only half his mind on things these days. He was the object of sincere sympathy. Edna Howard had not been universally liked – she was too wild a bird to be accepted in the Caxley hen-runs – but the marriage had been a happy one, and it was sad to see Sep so bereft.

Kathy was the one who gave him most comfort. If only Jim had been alive, Sep thought to himself! But Jim, his firstborn, lay somewhere in Ypres, and Leslie, his second son, was also lost to him. They had not met since Leslie left Winnie and went to live in the south-west with the woman of his choice.

Sep would have been desolate indeed without Kathy and Bertie's company. He spent most of his evenings there when the shop was closed, sitting quietly in a corner taking comfort from the children and the benison of a happy home. But he refused to sleep there, despite pressing invitations. Always he returned through the dark streets to the market square, passing the bronze statue of good Queen Victoria, before mounting the stairs to his lonely bedroom.

As the days grew longer the news became more and more sombre. The invasion of neutral Norway in April 1940 angered Caxley and the rest of the country. The costly attempts to recapture Narvik from the enemy, in the weeks that followed, brought outspoken criticism of Mr Chamberlain's leadership. Events were moving with such savagery and speed that it was clear that the time had arrived for a coalition government, and on May 10 Mr Churchill became Prime Minister.

Earlier, on the same day, Hitler invaded Holland. The news was black indeed. Before long it was known that a large part of the British Army had retreated to Dunkirk. The question 'How long can France hold out?' was on everyone's lips.

'They'll never give in,' declared Bertie to Sep, one glorious June evening in his garden. 'I've seen the French in action. They'll fight like tigers.'

The roses were already looking lovely. It was going to be a long hot summer, said the weatherwise of Caxley, and they were to be proved right. It did not seem possible, as the two men paced the grass, that across a narrow strip of water a powerful enemy waited to invade their land.

'They'll never get here,' said Bertie robustly. 'Napoleon was beaten by the Channel and so will Hitler be. The Navy will see to that.'

'At times I half-hope they will get here,' said Sep with a flash of spirit. 'There will be a warm welcome! I've never known people so spoiling for an encounter.'

Bertie was enrolled as a Local Defence Volunteer, soon to be renamed the Home Guard, and enjoyed his activities. One day, he hoped, he would return to army duties, but meanwhile there was plenty to organize in the face of imminent invasion.

Edward, now commissioned, had been posted to a squadron of Bomber Command in the north of England and was engaged in night bombing. Dickie Bridges was one of his crew. His letters showed such elation of spirit that the family's fears for him were partly calmed. Edward, it was plain, was doing exactly what he wanted to do – he was flying, he was in the thick of things, he was at the peak of his powers and deeply happy. The mention of a girl called Angela became more frequent. She was a Waaf on the same station and Winnie surmised that much of Edward's happiness came from her propinquity.

On a glorious hot June day, while haymaking was in full spate in the fields around Caxley and children refreshed themselves by splashing in the river Cax, the black news came over the radio that France had fallen. Joan Howard heard it in a little paper shop near the nursery school at dinner time. The old man who kept the shop beckoned her to the other side of the counter, and she stood, holding aside a hideous bead curtain which screened the tiny living-room from the shop, listening to the unbelievable news. She grew colder and colder. What would happen now?

The old man switched off the set when the announcement was over and turned to face her. To Joan's amazement his expression was buoyant.

'Now we're on our own,' he exclaimed with intense satisfaction. 'Never trusted them froggies for all old Winston said. We're better off without 'em, my dear. What was you asking for? *The Caxley Chronicle?* Thank you, dear. That's threepence. And now I'm off to get me Dad's old shot-gun polished up!'

She returned up the steep hill to the nursery school with the dreadful news. Miss Schmidt, the Viennese warden, always so gay and elegant, seemed to crumple into a frail old lady when Joan told her what she had heard.

'He is unbeatable,' she cried, and covered her face with her hands. Joan remembered the man in the paper shop and felt courage welling up in her.

'Rubbish!' she said stoutly. 'He's got us to reckon with. We'll never give in!'

'That is what my people said,' Miss Schmidt murmured, 'and the Poles and the Dutch. All of us – and now the French. The devil himself is with that man. He will rule the world.'

'You must not think that!' cried Joan. 'You know what the Prime Minister has said: "We'll fight on for years, if necessary alone," and it's true! We've all the Empire behind us. We can't lose, we can't!'

A child came up at this moment clamouring urgently for attention, and Miss Schmidt wiped away her tears and returned to her duties. But Joan could see that she could not believe that there was any hope for this small island where she had found brief refuge.

As for Joan herself, in some strange way her spirits grew more buoyant as the day wore on. Walking home that afternoon, through the brilliant sunshine, the confident words of the old man echoed in her ears: 'Now we're on our own. Better off without 'em, my dear!' They were as exhilarating as a marching song.

All Caxley seemed to share her mood, she discovered during the next few days. There was a fierce joy in the air, the relish of a fight.

'I'm sharpening up my filleting knife,' said Bill Petty at the fish stall in the market. The son of fat Mrs Petty, now dead, who had served there for years, Bill was a cripple who could never hope to see active service. His gaiety was infectious.

'I'll crown that Hitler with a jerry!' cried his neighbour at the crockery stall. 'Very suitable, don't you think?'

The spirit of Caxley was typical of the whole nation, roused, alert and ready to fight. As Doctor Johnson said: 'When a man knows he is going to be hanged in a fortnight, it concentrates his mind wonderfully.' Caxley concentrated to the full. Feverishly, defence plans went forward, old weapons were unearthed from cupboards and attics, and everyone intended to make it a fight to the finish.

'The Pry Minister,' said the B.B.C. announcer, 'will speak to the nation at hah-past nine tonight.' And the nation, listening, rejoiced to hear that brave belligerent voice saying: 'What has happened in France makes no difference to our actions and purpose. We have become the sole champions now in arms to defend the world cause. We shall fight on unconquerable until the curse of Hitler is lifted from the brows of mankind. We are sure that in the end all will come right.'

And somehow, despite the disaster of Dunkirk, the shortage of weapons, and the acknowledged might of the enemy, the people felt sure that all would come right.

It was two days later that a letter arrived at Rose Lodge from Edward. It was short and to the point.

Angela and I have just got engaged. So happy. Will bring her down to see you next weekend.
Love to you all,<br>Edward.

# EDWARD IN LOVE

She would never do, thought Winnie, gazing at Angela. She would never do at all. And yet, what was to be done about it? There was Edward, his dark eyes – so like his father's – fixed upon the girl, and his face wearing the expression which her mother so aptly described as 'the-cat's-got-at-the-cream'.

The memory of her own disastrous infatuation rushed at her from across the years. Was Edward about to make such an error of judgement? Or was she herself over-sensitive to the circumstances?

She tried to rationalize her feelings as she poured tea in the drawing-room at Rose Lodge. After all, she did not really know the girl. She must have faith in Edward's judgement. He was twenty-three, quite old enough to know his own mind. He was certainly very much in love, by the look of things. But – was she?

It was impossible to tell from Angela's cool, polite demeanour. She was small and very fair, with the neat good looks which would remain unchanged for many years. Just so had Winnie's mother been, trim and upright, and only recently had come the grey hair and wrinkles of old age to mar the picture. Old Mrs North's sharp blue eyes were now assessing the girl before them and

Winnie wondered what she would have to say when at last they were free to speak together.

She did not have long to wait. Edward took Angela to meet Bertie and Kathy and to show her something of Caxley. Winnie and her mother washed up the rarely-used fragile best china while their tongues wagged. Old Mrs North was surprisingly dispassionate. She loved Edward dearly and Winnie quite expected fierce criticism of his choice.

'Seems a ladylike sort of gal,' declared the old lady, dexterously exploring the inside of the teapot with the linen towel. 'And got her head screwed on, I don't doubt.'

'That's what worries me a bit,' confessed Winnie. 'Do you think she's in love with him? I think Edward's rather romantic, for all his shyness.'

'Hardly surprising,' commented her mother dryly. 'And I'd sooner see the girl level-headed about this business than getting foolishly infatuated. Let's face it, Winnie – we've seen what happens in that sort of situation in our own family.'

Winnie flushed. It was all so true, and yet, despite the wisdom of her mother's words, the nagging doubt remained. Was this girl the sort who could make Edward happy? She could only hope so.

They were married in August in a little grey church in the village by the aerodrome. Winnie and Joan had a nightmarish railway journey involving many changes and delays. They were the only representatives of Edward's family, for Bertie was now back in the army, blissfully happy in charge of fleets of army lorries at a maintenance unit. Kathy could not leave her family, and Sep and Robert were inextricably tied up with their business commitments.

Angela's mother was there. Her husband had left her some years before, but she was in the company of a prosperous-looking sixty-year-old who was introduced as 'a very dear friend'. Winnie disliked both on sight. Angela's mother was an older edition of the daughter, taut of figure, well dressed, with curls of unnaturally bright gold escaping from the smart forward-tilting hat. Her fashionable shoes, with their thick cork soles and heels, made Winnie's plain court shoes look very provincial. She sported a marcasite brooch in the shape of a basket of flowers on the lapel of her grey flannel suit, and spoke to Joan and Winnie in a faintly patronizing way which they both found intolerable.

She had travelled from Pinner in the friend's car, and Winnie would dearly have loved to inquire about the source of the petrol for this journey, but common decency forbade it.

The service was simple, the wedding breakfast at the local public house was informal, and the pair left for a two-day honeymoon somewhere in the Yorkshire dales. On their return the bridegroom would continue his bombing of Wilhelmshaven, Kiel or Bremen. How idiotic and unreal it all seemed, thought Winnie, making her way back to the station. The only real crumb of comfort was the memory of Edward's face, alight with happiness.

The golden summer wore on, and the blue skies above Caxley and the southern counties were criss-crossed with trails and spirals of silver vapour as the Battle of Britain raged in the air above the island. This was truly a battle for life and freedom as opposed to death and slavery at the hands of the Nazis. Across the channel the enemy amassed his armies of invasion, and by night and day sent waves of bombers to attack London and the south-east. The achievements of the R.A.F. gave the nation unparalleled hope of ultimate victory – long though it might be in coming.

The raids now began in earnest. The phoney war was at an end and the evacuees again began to stream from the stricken towns. Many of them spent the rest of the war away from their own homes. Many had no homes to return to. Many adopted the town of their refuge, grew up, married and became happy countrymen for the rest of their lives.

Sep's six boys had been found new billets when Edna died. Now he was anxious to have at least two back with him, despite the fact that his household help was sketchy. It was old Mrs North who thought of Miss Taggerty as housekeeper.

Miss Taggerty, almost as old as Sep, had once been in charge of Bender North's kitchenware department. She retired to look after an exasperating old father who was bed-ridden when being watched and remarkably spry on his pins when not, and who lived until the age of ninety-seven in a state of ever-growing demand. On his death, his cottage was due for demolition and poor, plain Miss Taggerty was to be made homeless.

The family had been anxious about Sep for some time. Joan very often called in to see her grandfather on the way home from school. He was touchingly grateful for her visits and Joan grew to love him, during this summer, more deeply than ever before. Bit by bit she began to realize how much Edna had meant to this lonely old man.

They sat together one hot afternoon in the little yard by the bakehouse, and Sep spoke of his lost wife. On the grey cobbles, near their outstretched legs, a beautiful peacock butterfly settled, opening and closing its bright powdery wings in the sunshine.

'Edna was like that,' said Sep in a low voice, almost as if he spoke to himself. 'As bright and lovely. I never cease to wonder that she settled with me – someone as humdrum and grey as that old cobblestone there. She could have had anyone in the world, she was so gay and pretty. I'd nothing to give her.'

'Perhaps,' said Joan, 'she liked to be near something solid and enduring, just as that butterfly does. If you are fragile and volatile then you are attracted to something stable. Surely that's why you and Grandma were so happy. You gave each other what the other lacked.'

'Maybe, maybe!' agreed Sep absently. There was a little pause and then he turned to look at his grandchild.

'You're a wise girl,' he said. 'Stay wise. Particularly when you fall in love, Joan. You need to consult your head as well as your heart when you start to think of marrying – and so many people will give you advice. Listen to them, but let your own heart and head give you the final answer.'

'I will,' promised Joan.

Later she was to remember this conversation. And Sep, with infinite sadness, was to remember it too.

Meanwhile, it was arranged for Miss Taggerty to take up her abode at Sep's house. The family was relieved to think that Sep would be properly looked after at last. With winter approaching, such things as well-aired sheets, good fires and a hot steak and kidney pudding made from rationed meat now and again, were matters of some domestic importance. With Miss Taggerty in the market square house the two evacuee boys could return, and Sep would be glad to feel that he was doing his war-time bit as well as having the pleasure of young company. As for Miss Taggerty, her cup of happiness was full. Used to a life of service, a gentle master such as Sep was a god indeed after the Moloch of her late father.

The winter of 1940 was indeed a bitter one. The war grew fiercer. Britain stood alone, at bay, the hope of the conquered nations and the inspiration of those who would later join in the struggle. The weather was unduly cold, fuel was short and food too. In Caxley, as elsewhere, this Christmas promised to be a bleak one.

But December brought one great glow of hope. The Lend-Lease Bill was prepared for submission to the United States' Congress. It meant that Britain could shape long-term plans of defence and attack with all the mighty resources of America behind her. It was a heart-warming thought in a chilly world.

Rose Lodge was to be the rendezvous for as many members of the Howard and North families as could manage it that Christmas. It looked as though it might be the last time that they would meet there, for, with the renewal of fighting, the question of turning the house into a nurses' hostel once again cropped up. This time it seemed most probable that it would be needed early in the New Year, and Winnie and her mother planned to move into the top floor of their old home, now

Edward's, in the market square, for the duration of the war. At the moment, Robert was being allowed to use the flat as storage space. The thought of moving out his supplies was something of a headache but, as Sep pointed out rather sternly, it must be done.

Edward and Angela arrived late on Christmas Eve. He had three days' leave and they had been lucky enough to get a lift down in a brother officer's car, three jammed in the back and three in the front. They were to return in the same fashion on Boxing Night.

They were in great good spirits when they burst in at the door. It was almost midnight but old Mrs North insisted on waiting up and the two women had a tray of food ready by the fire.

'If only I had a lemon,' cried Winnie, pouring out gin and tonic for the pair, 'I think I miss lemons and oranges more than anything else. And Edward always says gin and tonic without lemon is like a currant bun with no currants!'

'Not these days, mum,' said Edward stoutly. 'Gin alone, tonic alone would be marvellous. To have the two together in one glass in war-time is absolutely perfect.'

'And how do you find domestic life?' Winnie asked her daughter-in-law.

'Wonderful, after those awful days in the W.A.A.F.,' said Angela. 'I potter about in my own time, and it's lovely to compare notes with the other girls who pop in sometimes when they're off-duty.'

She went on to describe the two rooms in which she and Edward now lived in the village near the aerodrome. Life in the services had obviously never appealed to Angela and her present circumstances, though cramped and somewhat lonely, were infinitely preferable.

'If only Edward hadn't to go on those ghastly raids,' claimed his wife: 'I stay up all night sometimes, too worried to go to bed. Luckily, there's a phone in the house, and I ring up the mess every so often to see if he's back.'

'You'd do better to go straight to bed with some hot milk,' observed Winnie. 'It would be better for you and far better for Edward too, to know that you were being sensible. It only adds to his worries if he thinks you are miserable.'

'I'm surprised you are allowed to ring up,' said Mrs North.

'Oh, they don't exactly *like* it,' said Angela, 'but what do they expect?'

Edward changed the subject abruptly. He had tried to argue with Angela before on much the same lines, and with as little effect.

'Shall we see all the family tomorrow?'

'Bertie and Kathy and the children are coming to tea. They're bringing your grandfather too. He misses Grandma, particularly at Christmas, and they will all be together for Christmas dinner at Bertie's.'

'And there's just a chance,' added his grandmother North, 'that Aunt Mary may look in. She starts in pantomime one day this week, and may be able to come over for the day.'

Edward stretched himself luxuriously.

'It's wonderful to be back,' he said contentedly. 'Nowhere like Caxley. I can't wait for this bloody war to be over to get back again.'

'Language, dear!' rebuked his grandmother automatically, rising to go up to bed.

Before one o'clock on Christmas morning all the inhabitants of Rose Lodge were asleep.

All but one.

Edward lay on his back, his hands clasped behind his head, staring at the ceiling. Beside him Angela slept peacefully. He was having one of his 'black half-hours' as he secretly called them. What hopes had he of survival? What slender chances of returning to Caxley to live? Losses in Bomber Command were pretty hair-raising, and likely to become worse. He could view the thing fairly dispassionately for himself, although the thought of death at twenty-four was not what he looked for. But for Angela? How would she fare if anything happened to him? Thank God there were no babies on the way at the moment. He'd seen too many widows with young children recently to embark lightly on a family of his own.

The memory of his last raid on Kiel came

back to him with sickening clarity. They had encountered heavy anti-aircraft fire as they approached their target and the Wellington had been hit. Luckily not much damage was done. They dropped their load and Edward wheeled for home. But several jagged pieces of metal, razor-sharp, had flown across the aircraft from one side to the other, and Dickie Bridges was appallingly cut across the face and neck.

One of the crew had been a first-year medical student when he joined up, and tied swabs across a spouting artery and staunched the blood as best he could. Nevertheless, Dickie grew greyer and greyer as the Wellington sped back to base and it was obvious that something was hideously wrong with his breathing. Some obstruction in the throat caused him to gasp with a whistling sound which Edward felt he would remember until his dying day.

As they circled the aerodrome he was relieved to see the ambulance – known, grimly, as 'the blood cart' – waiting by the runway. Sick and scared, Edward touched down as gently as he could and watched Dickie carried into the ambulance. He knew, with awful certainty, that he would never see him alive again.

Dickie Bridges died as they were getting him ready for a blood transfusion, and next day Edward sat down with a heavy heart and wrote to his crippled mother. He had been her only child.

Damn all wars! thought Edward turning over violently in bed. If only he could be living in the market square, sharing his flat with Angela, starting a family, flying when he wanted to, pottering about with his friends and family in Caxley – what a blissful existence it would be!

And here he was, on Christmas morning too, full of rebellion when he should be thinking of peace and goodwill to all men. Somehow it hardly fitted in with total war, Edward decided sardonically.

He thought of all the other Christmas mornings he had spent under this roof, a pillowcase waiting at the end of the bed, fat with knobbly parcels and all the joy of Christmas Day spread out before him. They had been grand times.

Would this be the last Christmas for him? He put the cold thought from him absolutely. His luck had held so far. It would continue. It was best to live from day to day, 'soldiering on', as they said. Enough that it was Christmas time, he was in Caxley, and with Angela!

He pitched suddenly into sleep as if he were a pebble thrown into a deep pond. Outside, in the silent night, a thousand stars twinkled above the frost-rimed roofs of the little town of Caxley.

# THE MARKET SQUARE AGAIN

The New Year of 1941 arrived, and the people of Caxley, in company with the rest of the beleaguered British, took stock and found some comfort. The year which had passed gave reason for hope. Britain had held her own. Across the Atlantic the United States was arming fast and sending weapons in a steady stream to the Allied forces.

Even more cheering was the immediate news from Bardia in North Africa where the Australians were collecting twenty thousand Italian prisoners after one of the decisive battles in the heartening campaign which was to become known as the Desert Victory.

'The longer we hangs on the more chance we has of licking 'em!' pronounced an old farmer, knocking out his cherrywood pipe on the plinth of Queen Victoria's statue in the market square. He bent painfully and retrieved the small ball of spent tobacco which lay on the cobbles, picked one or two minute strands from it and replaced them carefully in his pipe.

'Not that we've got cause to get *careless*, mark you,' he added severely to his companion, who was watching the stubby finger ramming home the treasure trove. 'We've got to harbour our resources like Winston said – like what I'm doin' now – and then be ready to give them Germans what for whenever we gets the chance.'

And this, in essence, was echoed by the whole nation. 'Hanging on,' was the main thing, people told each other, and putting up with short commons as cheerfully as possible. It was not easy. As the months went by, 'making-do-and-mending' became more and more depressing, and sometimes well-night impossible. Another irritating feature of war-time life was the unbearable attitude of some of those in posts of officialdom.

It was Edward who noticed this particularly on one of his rare leaves in Caxley. It occurred one Saturday afternoon when the banks were closed and he needed some ready money. Luckily he had his Post Office savings book with him and thrust his way boisterously through the swing doors, book in hand. Behind the counter stood a red-haired girl whose protruding teeth rivalled Miss Taggerty's.

Edward remembered her perfectly. They had attended the same school as small children and he had played a golliwog to her fairy doll in the Christmas concert one year. On this occasion, however, she ignored his gay greeting, and thrust a withdrawal form disdainfully below the grille, her face impassive. Edward scribbled diligently and pushed it back with his book, whereupon the girl turned back the pages importantly in order to scrutinize the signature in the front and compare it with that on the form. For Edward, impatient to be away, it was too much.

'Come off it, Foof-teeth!' he burst out in exasperation, using the nickname of their schooldays. And only then did she melt enough to give him a still-frosty smile with the three pound notes.

There were equally trying people in Caxley, and elsewhere, who attained positions of petty importance and drove their neighbours to distraction: air raid wardens who seemed to relish every inadvertent chink of light in the black-out curtains, shop assistants rejoicing in the shortage of custard-powder, bus conductors harrying sodden queues, all added their pinpricks to the difficulties of everyday living, and these people little knew that such irritating officiousness would be remembered by their fellow-citizens for many years to come, just as the many little kindnesses, also occurring daily, held their place as indelibly in their neighbours' memories. Friends, and enemies, were made for life during war-time.

Howard's Restaurant continued to flourish despite shortages of good quality food stuffs which wrung Sep's heart. Robert failed his medical examination when his call-up occurred. Defective eyesight and some chest weakness sent him back to running the restaurant. Secretly, he was relieved. He had dreaded the discipline and the regulations almost more than the dangers of active service. He was content to plough along his familiar furrow, fraught though it was with snags and pitfalls, and asked only to be left in peace. He said little to his father about his feelings, but Sep was too wise not to know what went on in his son's head.

The boy was a disappointment to him, Sep admitted to himself. Sometimes he wondered why his three sons had brought so much unhappiness in their wake. Jim's death in the First World War had taken his favourite from him. Leslie, the gay lady-killer, had betrayed his trust and vanished westward to live with someone whom Sep still thought of as 'a wanton woman', despite her subsequent marriage to his son.

And now, Robert. Without wife or child, curiously secretive and timid, lacking all forms of courage, it seemed, he appeared to Sep a purely negative character. He ran the restaurant ably, to be sure, but he lacked friends and had no other interests in the town. Perhaps, if marriage claimed him one day, he would come to life. As it was he continued his way, primly and circumspectly, a spinsterish sort of fellow, with a streak of petty spite to which Sep was not blind.

His greatest comfort now was Kathy. He saw more of her now than ever, for Bertie was away in the army, and she and the children were almost daily visitors to the house in the market square. She grew more like her dear mother, thought Sep, with every year that passed. She had the same imperishable beauty, the flashing dark eyes, the grace of movement and dazzling smile which would remain with her throughout her life.

Yes, he was lucky to have such a daughter – and such wonderful grandchildren! He loved them all, but knew in his secret heart that it was Edward who held pride of place. There was something of Leslie – the *best* of Leslie, he liked to think – something of the Norths, and a strong dash of himself in this beloved grandson. He longed to see children of Edward's before he grew too old to enjoy their company. Did his wife, that beautiful but rather distant Angela, really know what a fine man she had picked? Sometimes Sep had his doubts, but times were difficult for everyone, and for newly-weds in particular. With the coming of peace would come the joy of a family, Sep felt sure.

And for Joan too, he hoped. She was a North, despite her name, if ever there was one, and the Norths were made for domesticity. There flashed into the old man's mind a picture of his dead friend Bender North, sitting at ease in his Edwardian drawing-room, above the shop which was now Howard's Restaurant. He saw him now, contented and prosperous, surveying the red-plush furniture, the gleaming sideboard decked with silver, smoking his Turk's-head pipe, at peace with the world. Just as contentedly had Bertie settled down with Kathy. He prayed that Joan, in her turn, might find as felicitous a future in a happy marriage. It was good, when one grew old, to see the younger generations arranging their affairs, and planning a world which surely would be better than that in which Sep had grown up.

Joan was indeed planning her future, unknown to her family. She was still absorbed in her work at the nursery school and as the months of war crept by it became apparent that the chances of joining the W.A.A.F. became slighter.

For one thing, the numbers at the school increased rapidly. As local factories stepped-up their output more young women were needed, and their children were left in the care of the school. And then the Viennese warden was asked to take over the job of organizing nursery work for the whole county, and Joan, trembling a little at such sudden responsibility, was put in charge.

She need not have worried. Despite her youth, she was well-trained, and had had varied experience. Allied to this, her equable North temperament and her genuine affection for the children, made her ideally suited to the post. Two women had been added to the staff, one of them being Maisie Hunter who had arrived at the beginning of the war as an evacuee at Rose Lodge and who had remained in the neighbourhood. She was a tower of strength to Joan. The second teacher was a wispy young girl straight from college, anxious to do the right thing, and still with the words of her child-psychology lecturer ringing in her ears. Joan could only hope that face-to-face encounters with healthy three-year-olds would in time bring her down to earth a little, and give her confidence.

All this made Joan realize that her duty really lay with these young children and the job with which she had been landed. In some ways she regretted it. Her dream of being posted somewhere near Edward, perhaps even learning to fly one day, was doomed to fade. Nevertheless, this job was one equally valuable, and one which she knew she could tackle. It meant too that she could keep an eye on her mother and grandmother. Winnie was more active than ever, it seemed, but there were times when old Mrs North looked suddenly frail, and her memory, until now so acute, was often at fault. The oven would be left on, telephone messages were forgotten, spectacles and bags mislaid a dozen times a day and, worse still, the autocratic old lady would never admit that any of these little mishaps was her own fault. Physically, she was as active as ever, mounting the steep stairs to the flat in the market square as lightly as she had done when she lived there as mistress of the house so many years before.

All three women found the quarters somewhat cramped after Rose Lodge, but they all enjoyed living again in the heart of Caxley, close to their neighbours, and with the weekly market to enliven the scene each Thursday. They were handy too for the shops and for Sep's restaurant down below where they frequently called for a meal.

They found too that they were admirably placed to receive visits from their family and friends. Buses were few and far between, but the market square was a main shopping point, and friends and relations from the villages could call easily. Old Mrs North's sister, Ethel Miller, whose husband farmed at Beech Green, frequently came to see them bearing farm eggs, butter, an occasional chicken or duck – treasures indeed in wartime.

It was her Aunt Ethel who first introduced Michael to Joan. He was one of three junior army officers billeted at the farm, and Joan had heard a little about them all. They seemed to be a cheerful high-spirited trio and her aunt was devoted to them – indeed, so fulsome was she in her praise, that Joan had tended to think that their charms must be considerably overrated.

'Michael is picking me up at six o'clock,' said Aunt Ethel, glancing at the timepiece on the mantelpiece. She had been ensconced on the sofa when Joan came in from school at tea-time.

'He's had to collect some equipment from the station in the truck,' she explained, 'and offered me a lift.'

At ten past six they heard the sound of footsteps pounding up the stairs and Joan opened the door to admit the young man. He was full of apologies for being late, but he did not look particularly downcast, Joan observed. Aunt Ethel, anxious to get back to the family and the farm, made hurried farewells, and the two vanished after a few brief civilities. Joan, in spite of herself, was most impressed with the stranger.

He was exceptionally tall, a few inches over six feet, slender and dark. He had grey bright eyes with thick black lashes, and his face was lantern-jawed and pale. He was an Irishman, Joan knew, and he looked it. In the few words which he had spoken, Joan had recognized the soft brogue and the intonation full of Irish charm. A heart-breaker, if ever there was one, commented Joan amusedly to herself!

They did not meet again for some time, but one Saturday early in October, Joan offered to take some wool to the farm for her aunt.

'It will do me good to get some exercise,' she said, trundling out her bicycle from the shed where Bender had once kept mangles and dustbins, buckets and baths, in the old days.

It was a still misty day. Cobwebs were slung along the hedges like miniature hammocks. Droplets hung on the ends of wet twigs. There was a smell of autumn in the air, a poignant mixture of dead leaves, damp earth and the whiff of a distant bonfire.

Halfway to Beech Green a sharp hill caused Joan to dismount. She stood still for a moment to get back her breath. Above her a massive oak tree spread gnarled wet arms. Looking up into its intricacies of pattern against the soft pale sky she noticed dozens of cobwebs draped liked scraps of grey chiffon between the rough bark of the sturdy trunk and the branches. Far away, hidden in the mist, a train hooted. Near at hand, a blackbird scrabbled among papery brown leaves beneath the hedge. Otherwise silence enveloped the girl and she realized, with a shock, how seldom these days she enjoyed complete solitude.

What a long time it was too, she thought, since she had consciously observed such everyday natural miracles as the cobwebs and the blackbird's liquid eye! Engrossed with the children and their mothers, walking to and from the nursery school along the pavements of Caxley, restricted by war from much outside activity, she had quite forgotten the pleasure which flowers and trees, birds and animals had subconsciously supplied. She free-wheeled down the long hill to the farm, exhilarated by her unaccustomed outing.

Her aunt was busy making a new chicken-run and, with a quickening of the heart, Joan saw that Michael was wielding the mallet which drove in the stakes.

'You dear girl,' exclaimed Aunt Ethel, proffering a cold damp cheek to be kissed, while her fingers ripped open the package. 'Four whole ounces! I can't believe it! Now I shall be able to knit Jesse a good thick pair of winter socks. How on earth did Hilda manage it?'

'Sheer favouritism,' replied Joan. 'It was under-the-counter stuff, and passed over with much secrecy, I understand. They only had two pounds of wool altogether, Grandma said, and you had to be a real old blue-blooded Caxleyite to nobble an ounce or two.'

Michael laughed at this, and Joan found him more attractive than ever.

'Now hold the end of this wire,' directed Aunt Ethel, returning to the business in hand, 'and we'll be done in no time. Then you must stop and have lunch. It's rabbit casserole with lots of carrots.'

'S'posed to keep off night-blindness, whatever that is,' said Michael jerkily, between powerful blows with the mallet.

When the job was done and the excellent rabbit demolished, Michael and Joan sat in the warm farm kitchen and talked. Uncle Jesse was in the yard attempting to repair a wiring fault in his ancient Ford, while Aunt Ethel had gone upstairs 'to sort the laundry', she explained, although Joan knew very well that she was having the nap which she refused to admit she took every afternoon.

Michael talked easily. He told her about his home in Dublin and his family there.

'My old man keeps a hotel. Nothing in the five-star range, you know. Just a little place where the commercials stay overnight – but we've a quiet decent little house there and a grand garden.'

He had two sisters and a brother, he told her. His mother was an invalid, and he wanted to get back soon to see her.

'And what do you do,' asked Joan, 'when you're not in the Army?'

'I'm not too sure,' answered Michael. 'You see, I'd just got my degree at Trinity College when war broke out. Maybe I'll teach. I read modern languages. Oh, there now, I can't tell you what I'll do, and that's the truth!'

Joan was intrigued with the way the last word came out as 'troot'. Despite his vagueness about the future, it was apparent that he intended to do something worthwhile. She told him a little about her own work and he seemed deeply interested.

'You're lucky,' he said. 'You know where you're going. Maybe I'll know too before long, but let's get the war over first, I think. Somehow, it's difficult to make plans when you may be blown to smithereens tomorrow.'

He spoke cheerfully, his wide smile making a joke of the grim words.

'I wish I could see you home,' he said when at last Joan rose to go. 'But I'm on duty in half an hour. Can I ring you one day soon? Are you ever free?'

'I'm completely free,' Joan said.

'Good!' replied the young man with evident satisfaction.

They walked together to the front door of the farmhouse. Joan's dilapidated bicycle stood propped against the massive door-scraper which had served generations of muddy-booted Millers.

Across the lawn a copper beech tree stood against the grey-fawn sky, like some old sepia photograph, framed in the oblong of the doorway.

'It's a grand country,' said Michael softly.

'Lovelier than Ireland?'

'Ah, I'm not saying that! Have you never been?'

'Never.'

'You must go one day when the war's over. I'll look forward to showing it to you.'

'That would be lovely,' said Joan, primly polite. She mounted the bicycle and smiled her farewells. He saluted very smartly, eyes twinkling, and watched her ride away.

She reported on her visit to her mother and grandmother as they sat by the fire that evening, saying little about Michael. She was more deeply attracted than she cared to admit, and felt that she could not face any family probings.

Old Mrs North's sharp eye, however, missed nothing.

'An attractive young man, that Michael,' she

said, briskly tugging at her embroidery needle. 'Even if he is Irish.'

Joan smiled.

'Pity he's a Roman Catholic,' continued the old lady. 'Off to seven o'clock mass as regular as clockwork, Ethel says. But there,' she added indulgently, 'I expect it keeps him out of mischief.'

Joan nodded. But her smile had gone.

## THE INVASION

Edward had been posted yet again. This time itwas to a station in Wales where he would be a staff pilot, instructing others in the art of flying bombers. This was a rest period, for six months or possibly longer, between operational tours.

Angela was more than usually disgruntled at the move. She insisted on accompanying her husband wherever he might be, and was beginning to get heartily sick of other people's houses and unending domestic problems. As the war dragged on, she became steadily more discontented with her lot, and Edward was sincerely sorry for her. He knew how long the days were, cooped in two rooms, in someone else's home. He realized, only too well, the anxiety she suffered when he was on operations. And he was beginning to see that Angela had very few inner resources to give her refreshment and strength to combat her tedium.

She seemed to spend most of her time in the company of other young wives as bored as she was herself. They met for innumerable coffee parties and games of bridge. Edward had suggested more fruitful ways of spending the time. There was plenty of voluntary work to be done, helping in hospitals, schools, A.R.P. centres and so on but Angela's answer had been disturbing and illuminating.

'I married you to get out of the W.A.A.F. Why the devil should I put my head into another noose?'

It was not very reassuring to a newly-married man, and as the months lengthened into years Edward began to realize that Angela had meant every word of that remark. Perhaps they should have started a family, foolhardy though it seemed. Would things have been more satisfactory? He doubted it. Edward was too wise to pin his hopes on motherhood as a panacea to all marital ills, and he had observed other young couples' problems with babies in wartime. It was difficult enough to obtain accommodation without children. Those who had them were definitely at a disadvantage.

No, thought Edward, they had been right to wait. But would the time ever come when they both looked forward to children? With a heavy heart, he began to face the fact that Angela might have waited too long.

It was at the end of May when Edward and Angela made their next visit to Caxley.

'No family yet then?' Mrs North greeted them, with devastating directness. 'Why's that?'

Angela pointedly ignored the question. Edward laughed, hugged his diminutive grandmother and pointed out of the window to the market square.

'That partly,' he replied.

A steady flow of army transport was travelling across the square heading south to the ports. Lorries, armoured cars and tanks had been pouring through Caxley for days now, and the thunder of their passage shook the old house and caused headaches among the inhabitants.

But there was no heart-ache. This, they knew, was the start of a great invasion – an invasion in reverse. The time had come when this mighty allied force could cross the Channel and begin the task of liberating oppressed Europe. Who would have thought it? they bellowed to each other, against the din. Four years ago it was the British Isles which awaited invasion! The tables were turned indeed.

Edward was now stationed within eighty miles of Caxley and was back on operational duty. He had no doubt that he would be busy bombing supply bases and cutting the communications of the retreating enemy. He should see plenty of activity, he told himself. It would be good to support an attacking army in Europe.

'Make no mistake,' he told his family, 'we're on the last lap now. Then back to Caxley and peace-time!'

That afternoon, while Angela was at the hairdresser's, he walked through the throbbing town to see Bertie who was also on brief leave. He found him pushing the lawn mower, his fair hair turning more and more ashen as the grey hairs increased, but still lissom in figure and with the same gentle good looks.

They greeted each other warmly.

'Kathy's out on some W.V.S. ploy,' said Bertie, 'and the children are still at school. Come and have a look at the river. It's quieter there than anywhere else in Caxley at the moment. But, by God, what a welcome sound, Edward, eh? Great days before us, my boy!'

It was indeed peaceful by the Cax. The shining water slipped along reflecting the blue and white sky. Here and there it was spangled with tiny white flowers which drifted gently to and fro with the current. On the towpath, across the river, a cyclist pedalled slowly by, and his reflection, upside down, kept pace with him swiftly and silently. The moment was timeless and unforgettable.

'Tell me,' said Bertie, 'has Joan said anything to you about Michael?'

'Not much,' replied Edward, startled from his reverie by something in his uncle's tone. 'Why, what's up?'

'They're very much in love,' said Bertie slowly. 'And to my mind would make a very good pair. He's a Catholic, of course, but it doesn't worry me. I wondered if it would complicate matters with the family.'

'Grandfather'd hate it,' admitted Edward bluntly. 'And probably Grandma North. I can't see anyone else losing much sleep over it. Surely, it's their affair.'

'I agree,' said Bertie. They paced the path slowly. Edward noticed that Bertie's limp was more accentuated these days and remembered, with a slight shock, that his uncle must now be over fifty.

'After all,' continued Edward ruminatively, 'you can't call the Norths a deeply religious family – and Joan and I, for all we're called Howard, take after the Norths in that way. I can't truthfully say I'm a believer, you know. There's too much to accept in church teaching – I boggle at a lot of it. But for those who really are believers, well, it's probably better to go the whole hog and be a Catholic, You know where you are, don't you?'

'Meaning what?' asked Bertie smiling at Edward's honest, if inelegant, reasoning.

'Well, if Joan is as luke-warm as I am, and yet she recognizes that Michael has something in his faith which means something to him, then she may be willing for the children to be brought up in the same way. I just don't know. I've never talked of such things with her.'

They turned in their tracks and made their way slowly back. A kingfisher, a vivid arrow of blue and green, streaked across the water and vanished into the tunnel made by the thick-growing chestnut trees.

'Lucky omen!' commented Bertie.

'In love or war?' asked Edward, gazing after it.

'Both, I predict,' said Bertie confidently, limping purposefully homeward.

It was at the end of that same week that Michael and Joan mounted the stairs to the flat and told Winnie and her mother that they were engaged.

Edward and Bertie were back on duty, Michael was moving to the coast the next day with his unit. The young couple did not blind themselves to the risks of the next few days. The casualties would be heavy, and it was likely that the army would bear the brunt of the attack. But nothing could dim their happiness, and Winnie and old Mrs North were glad to give them their blessing.

When at last Michael had gone and Joan returned, pink and a little damp-eyed from making her farewells, Mrs North spoke briskly the thoughts which were shared, but would have been left unuttered, by Winnie.

'Well, dear, I'm very happy for you. I've always liked Michael, as you know, and as long as you face the fact that there will be a new baby every twelve months or so I'm sure it will work out well. You'll stay C. of E. I suppose?'

'No, Grandma,' replied Joan composedly. 'I shall become a Roman Catholic, like all those babies-to-be.'

'Pity!' said the old lady. 'Well, you know your own business best, I suppose. Sleep well, and remember to take that ring off whenever you put your hands in water. Goodnight, dears.'

She put up her soft papery cheek to be kissed as usual, and went off to bed.

Winnie looked at her daughter. She looked tired out. Who wouldn't, thought Winnie, with all she had been through, and with Michael off to battle at first light? And yet there was a calmness about her which seemed unshakeable. Just so had she herself been when breaking the news of her engagement to Joan's father. Please, she prayed suddenly, let her marriage be happier than mine! And happier than Edward's! It was the first time, she realized suddenly, that she had admitted to herself that Edward's marriage was heading for the rocks. Were they all to be doomed to unhappiness with their partners?

She put the dark fear from her and kissed her daughter affectionately.

'Bed, my love,' she said.

It was Sep, of course, who felt it most. Joan told him the news herself the next day. She found him pottering about in his bakehouse, stacking tins and wiping the already spotless shelves.

She thought how little the place had changed since she was a child. The same great scrubbed table stood squarely in the middle of the red-tiled floor. The same comfortable warmth embraced one, and the same wholesome smell of flour and newly-baked bread pervaded the huge building. And Sep too, at first sight, seemed as little changed. Small, neat, quiet and deft in his movements, his grey hair was as thick as ever, his eyes as kindly as Joan always remembered them.

'Sit 'ee down, sit 'ee down,' cried Sep welcomingly, pulling forward a tall wooden stool. 'And what brings you here, my dear?'

Joan told him, twisting Michael's beautiful sapphire ring about her finger as she spoke. Sep heard her in silence to the end.

'I know you can't approve wholeheartedly, Grandpa,' said Joan, looking up at his grave face, 'but don't let it come between us, please.'

Sep sighed.

'Nothing can,' he said gently. 'You are part of my family, and a very dear part, as you know.

And you're a wise child, I've always said so. Do you remember how you comforted me when your dear grandmother died?'

'You asked me then to choose wisely when I got married,' nodded Joan. 'I remember it very well. Do you think that I've chosen unwisely after all?'

'You have chosen a good man; I have no doubt of that,' replied Sep. 'But I cannot be happy to see you embracing his faith. You know my feelings on the subject. It is a religion which I find absolutely abhorrent, battening on the poor and ignorant, and assuming in its arrogance that all other believers are heretics.'

'Michael would tell you that it is the one gleam of hope in the lives of many of those poor and ignorant people,' replied Joan.

'Naturally he would,' responded Sep shortly. 'He is a devout Catholic. He believes what he is told to believe.'

He turned away and stood, framed in the doorway, looking with unseeing eyes at the cobbled yard behind the bakehouse. The clock on the wall gave out its measured tick. Something in one of the ovens hissed quietly. To Joan the silence seemed ominous. Her grandfather wheeled round and came back to where she sat, perched high on the wooden stool.

'We'll say no more. There must be no quarrels between us two. You will do whatever you think is right, I know, without being swayed by people round you. But think, my dear, I beg of you. Think, and pray. There are your children to consider.'

'I have thought,' replied Joan soberly.

'And whatever your decision,' continued Sep, as though he had not heard her interjection, 'we shall remain as we've always been. I want you to feel that you can come to me at any time. Don't let anything – ever – come between us, Joan.'

She rose from the stool and bent to kiss the little man's forehead.

'Nothing can,' she assured him. 'Nothing, Grandpa.'

But as she crossed the market square, and paused by Queen Victoria's statue to let the wartime traffic thunder by, her heart was torn by the remembrance of Sep's small kind face, suddenly shrivelled and old. That she, who loved him so dearly, could have wrought such a change, was almost more than she could bear.

On the night of 5 June in that summer of 1944 a great armada sailed from the English ports along the channels already swept clear of mines. By dawn the next day the ships stood ready off the Normandy coast for the biggest amphibious operation of the war – the invasion of Europe.

Edward was engaged in attacking enemy coast-defence guns, flying a heavy bomber. As the first light crept across the sky, the amazing scene was revealed to him as he flew back to base. The line upon line of ships, great and small, might have been drawn up ready for a review. A surge of pride swept him as he looked from above. The fleet in all its wartime strength was an exhilarating sight. Edward, for one, had not the faintest doubt in his mind that by the end of this vital day victory would be within sight.

Excitement ran high in the country. News had just been received of the liberation of Rome under General Alexander's command, but people were agog to know what was going on across the strip of water which had so long kept their island inviolate.

At midday the Prime Minister gave welcome news to the House of Commons. 'An immense armada of upwards of four thousand ships, together with several thousand smaller craft, crossed the Channel,' he told them and went on to say that reports coming in showed that everything was proceeding according to plan. 'And what a plan!' he added.

It was the success of this vast enterprise, on sea and land simultaneously, which gripped the imagination of the country. Napoleon had been daunted by the Channel. Hitler, for all his threats, had been unable to cross it. The success of the allied British and American armies in this colossal undertaking was therefore doubly exciting.

The inhabitants of Caxley kept their radio sets switched on, eager to hear every scrap of news which came through. Joan longed to know where Michael was and how he was faring. There must have been heavy casualties, she knew, and the suspense was agonizing.

The Norths and Howards knew where their other fighting men were. Bertie was stationed not far from Poole, and Edward was based in Kent. They did not expect to hear or see much of the pair of them in these exciting times, but the fortunes of Michael, now somewhere in the thick of things in Normandy were the focus of their thoughts.

As the days went by they grieved for Joan watching anxiously for the postman's visits. There was sobering news during the next week, about stubborn enemy resistance at the town of Caen. It was apparent that failure to capture this key-point would mean that a large force of allied troops would be needed there for some time. Could the enemy make a come-back?

One sunny morning the longed-for letter arrived and Joan tore it open in the privacy of her bedroom. She read it swiftly.

My Darling Joan,

All's well here. Tough going, but not a scratch, and a grand set of chaps. We are constantly on the move – but in the right direction, Berlin-wards. The people here are being wonderful to us.

I can't wait to get home again. Look after yourself. I'll write again as soon as I get a chance.

All my love,<br>Michael

Joan sat down hard on the side of the bed and began to cry. There was a tap at the door and her grandmother looked in. Tears were rolling steadily down the girl's cheeks, splashing upon the letter in her hands.

A chill foreboding gripped the old lady. In a flash she remembered the dreadful day during the First World War when she had heard the news that Bertie was seriously wounded in hospital. The memory of that nightmare drive to see him was as fresh in her mind as if it had happened yesterday.

She advanced towards her granddaughter, arms outstretched to comfort.

'Oh, Joan,' she whispered. 'Bad news then?'

The girl, sniffing in the most unladylike way, held out the letter.

'No, Grandma,' she quavered. 'It's good news. He's safe.'

And she wept afresh.

# EDWARD AND ANGELA

It was the beginning of the end of the war, and everyone knew it. Perhaps this was the most hopeful moment of the long conflict. The free world still survived. Within a year Europe would be liberated, and two or three months later, hostilities would cease in the Far East. Meanwhile, a world which knew nothing yet of Belsen and Hiroshima, rejoiced in the victory which was bound to come.

It was the beginning of the end too, Edward realized, of his marriage. Things had gone from bad to worse. No longer could he blind himself with excuses for Angela's estrangement. Indifference had led to recriminations, petty squabbles, and now to an implacable malice on his wife's part. Edward, shaken to the core, had no idea how to cope with the situation now that things had become so bleakly impossible.

Any gesture of affection, any attempt on his part to heal the breach, was savagely rebuffed. Anything sterner was greeted with hysterical scorn. If he was silent he was accused of sulking, if he spoke he was told he was a bore.

It was about this time that an old admirer of Angela's appeared. She and Edward had been invited to a party at a friend's house. There was very little social life in the small Kentish town where they were then living, and Angela accepted eagerly. Edward preferred to be at home on the rare occasions when that was possible. He dreaded too the eyes which watched them, and knew that the break-up of their marriage was becoming all too apparent. But he went with good grace and secretly hoped that they would be able to get away fairly early.

It was a decorous, almost stuffy, affair. About twenty people, the local doctor and his wife, a schoolmaster, a few elderly worthies as well as one or two service couples, stood about the poorly-heated drawing-room and made falsely animated conversation. Their hostess was a large kindhearted lady swathed in black crêpe caught on the hip with a black satin bow. She was afflicted with deafness but courageously carried on loud conversations with every guest in turn. As the rest of the company raised their voices in order to make themselves heard, the din was overwhelming. Edward, overwrought and touchy, suddenly had a vision of the leafy tunnel of chestnut trees which arched above the Cax, and longed with all his soul to be there with only the whisper of the water in his ears.

As it was, he stood holding his weak whisky and water, his eyes smarting with smoke and his face frozen in a stiff mask of polite enjoyment. The doctor's wife was telling him a long and involved story about a daughter in Nairobi, of which Edward heard about one word in ten.

Across the room he could see Angela, unusually gay, talking to an army officer whom he had not seen before.

They certainly seemed to enjoy each other's company, thought Edward, with a pang of envy. How pretty Angela was tonight! If only she would look at him like that – so happily and easily! The tale of the Nairobi daughter wound on interminably, and just as Edward was wondering how on earth he could extricate himself, he saw Angela's companion look across, touch Angela's arm, and together they began to make their way towards him.

At the same moment the doctor's wife was claimed by a faded little woman in a droopy-hemmed stockinette frock. They pecked each other's cheeks and squawked ecstatically. Thankfully, Edward moved towards his wife.

'Can you believe it?' cried Angela, 'I've found Billy again, after all these years! Billy Sylvester, my husband.'

'How d'you do?' said the men together.

'Billy has digs at the doctor's,' Angela prattled on excitedly. Edward wondered if he had heard all about the daughter in Nairobi, and felt a wave of sympathy towards the newcomer.

'We used to belong to the same sports club years ago,' continued Angela, 'before Bill went into the army. Heavens, what a lot of news we've got to exchange!'

'Mine's pretty dull,' said Billy with a smile. He

began to talk to Edward, as the daughter of the house moved across to replenish their glasses. He had been in the town now for about a month it transpired, and was in charge of stores at his camp.

'Any chance of going overseas?' asked Edward.

'Not very likely,' replied Billy, 'I'm getting a bit long in the tooth, and my next move will be either up north or west, as far as I can gather.'

Edward watched him with interest, as they sipped amidst the din. He was probably nearing forty, squarely built, with a large rather heavy face, and plenty of sleek black hair. He spoke with a pleasing Yorkshire accent, and gave the impression of being a sound business man, which was indeed the case. He did not appear to be the sort of man who would flutter female hearts, but Angela's blue eyes were fixed upon him in such a challenging manner, that Edward wondered what lay hidden from him in the past. Probably nothing more serious than a schoolgirl's crush on the star tennis player at the club, he decided. Or, even more likely, yet another gambit to annoy an unwanted husband. He was getting weary of such pinpricks, he had to admit.

Nevertheless, he liked the fellow. He liked his air of unpretentious solidity, the fact that his deep voice could be heard clearly amidst the clamour around them, and the way in which he seemed oblivious of Angela's advances.

After some time, Edward saw one of his friends across the room. He was newly-married and his young shy wife was looking well out of her depth.

'Let's go and have a word with Tommy,' said Edward to Angela.

'You go,' she responded. 'I'll stay with Bill.'

And stay she did, much to the interest of the company, for the rest of the evening.

Edward saw very little of Billy Sylvester after that. Occasionally, they came across each other in the town, and on one bitterly cold morning they collided in the doorway of 'The Goat and Compasses'. Angela, Edward knew, had seen something of him, but he had no idea how often they met. Angela spoke less and less, but she had let out that Billy had parted from his wife before the war, and that he had two boys away at boarding school.

Air attacks in support of the Allied forces were being intensified and Edward was glad to have so much to occupy him. He had been promoted again, and was beginning to wonder if he would stay in the Air Force after the war. In some ways he wanted to. On the other hand the restrictions of service life, which he had endured cheerfully enough in war-time, he knew would prove irksome and certainly Angela would be against the idea. He was beginning to long for roots, a home, a family, something to see growing. In his more sanguine moments he saw Angela in the Caxley flat, refurbishing it with him, starting life afresh. Or perhaps buying a cottage near the town, on the hilly slopes towards Beech Green, say, or in the pleasant southern outskirts of Caxley near the village of Bent? And then the cold truth would press in upon him. In his heart of hearts he knew that there could never be a future with Angela. She had already left him. The outlook was desolate. Meanwhile, one must live from day to day, and let the future take care of itself.

He returned home one wet February afternoon to find the flat empty. This did not perturb him, as Angela was often out. He threw himself into an armchair and began to read the newspaper. Suddenly he was conscious of something unusual. There was no companionable ticking from Angela's little clock on the mantelpiece. It had vanished. No doubt it had gone to be repaired, thought Edward, turning a page. He looked at his watch. It had stopped. Throwing down the paper, he went into the bedroom to see the time by the bedside alarm clock. The door of the clothes cupboard stood open and there were gaps where Angela's frocks and coats had hung.

Propped against the table lamp was a letter. Edward felt suddenly sick. It had come at last. His hands trembled as he tore it open.

Dear Edward,
   Billy and I have gone away together. Don't try

to follow us. Nothing you can do or say will ever bring me back. I don't suppose you'll miss me anyway.

Angela

At least, thought Edward irrelevantly, she was honest enough not to add 'Love'. What was to be done? He thrust the letter into his pocket and paced up and down the bedroom. He must go after her, despite her message. She was his wife. She must be made to return.

He stopped short and gazed out into the dripping garden. The tree trunks glistened with rain. Drops pattered on the speckled leaves of a laurel bush, and a thrush shook its feathers below.

Why must she be made to return? He was thinking as Sep might think, he suddenly realized. Angela was not a chattel. And what sort of life could they hope to live if he insisted on it? It was best to face it. It was the end.

The thrush pounced suddenly and pulled out a worm from the soil. It struggled gamely, stretched into a taut pink rubbery line. The thrush tugged resolutely. Poor devil, thought Edward, watching the drama with heightened sensibilities. He knew how the worm felt – caught, and about to be finished. The bird gave a final heave. The worm thrashed for a moment on the surface and was systematically jabbed to death by the ruthless beak above. Just so, thought Edward, have I been wounded, and just so, watching the thrush gobble down its meal, have I been wiped out. He watched the thrush running delicately across the wet grass, its head cocked sideways, searching for another victim.

He threw himself upon the bed and buried his face in the coverlet. There was a faint scent of the perfume which Angela used and his stomach was twisted with sudden pain. One's body, it seemed, lagged behind one's mind when it came to parting. This was the betrayer – one's weak flesh. A drink was what he needed, but he felt unable to move, drained of all strength, a frail shell shaken with nausea.

Suddenly, as though he had been hit on the back of the head, he fell asleep. When he awoke, hours later, it was dark, and he was shivering with the cold. His head was curiously heavy, as though he were suffering from a hangover, but he knew, the moment that he awoke, what had caused this collapse. Angela had gone.

The world would never be quite as warm and fair, ever again.

Meanwhile, in Caxley, Joan was receiving instruction from the local Roman Catholic priest, much to her own satisfaction and to her grandfather's secret sorrow.

The wedding was planned for the end of April, when Michael expected leave, and would take place in the small shabby Catholic church at the northern end of Caxley.

Old Mrs North made no secret of her disappointment.

'I've always hoped for a family wedding at St Peter's,' she said regretfully to Joan. 'Your dear mother would have made a lovely bride. I so often planned it. The nave is particularly suitable for a wedding. I hoped Winnie would have a train. Nothing more dignified – in good lace, of course. And the flowers! They always look so beautiful at the entrance to the chancel. Lady Hurley's daughter looked a picture flanked by arum lilies and yellow roses! D'you remember, Winnie dear? It must have been in 1929. I suppose there's no hope of you changing your mind, dear, and having the wedding at dear old St Peter's?'

'None at all,' smiled Joan. 'Of course, if I'd met Michael four or five hundred years ago we should have been married in St Peter's. But thanks to Henry the Eighth I must make do with the present arrangements.'

'Now, that's a funny thing,' confessed her grandmother. 'It never occurred to me that St Peter's was once Roman Catholic! It really gives one quite a turn, doesn't it?'

Preparations went on steadily. Joan got together a sizeable quantity of linen and household goods. Kind friends and relatives parted with precious clothing coupons and she was able to buy a modest trousseau. Sep made the most elegant wedding cake consistent with war-time restrictions and embellished it, touchingly, with the decorations from his own wedding cake which Edna had treasured.

He had given Joan a generous dowry.

'You will want a house of your own one day,' he told her. 'This will be a start. I hope it won't be far from Caxley, my dear, but I suppose it depends on Michael. But I hope it won't be in Ireland. Too far for an old man like me to visit you.'

Joan could not say. Somehow she thought that Ireland would be her home in the future. As Sep said, it all depended on Michael.

One thing grieved her, in the midst of her hopeful preparations. Sep would be present at the reception, but he could not face the ceremony in the Catholic church. His staunch chapel principles would not allow him to put a foot over the threshold.

In the midst of the bustle came Edward's catastrophic news. Joan, herself so happy, was shocked and bewildered. The bond between Edward and herself was a strong one, doubly so perhaps, because they had been brought up without a father. She had never shared her mother's and grandmother's misgivings about Angela, for somehow she had felt sure that anyone must be happy with Edward, so cheerful, so dependable as he was. This blow made her suddenly unsure of her judgement. Loyalty to her brother made her put the blame squarely on Angela's shoulders. On the other hand, a small doubting voice reminded her of the old saw that it takes two to make a marriage.

Had Edward been at fault? Or was this tragedy just another side-effect of war? She prayed that she and Michael would be more fortunate.

Her mother took the news soberly and philosophically. She had known from the first that Angela would never do. Much as she grieved for Edward, it was better that they should part now, and she thanked Heaven that no children were involved in the parting.

It was old Mrs North, strangely enough, who seemed most upset. Normally, her tart good sense strengthened the family in times of crisis. This time she seemed suddenly old – unable to bear any more blows. The truth was that the ancient wound caused by Winnie's unhappy marriage to Leslie Howard, was opened again. With the controversial marriage of Joan imminent, the old lady's spirits drooped at this fresh assault. Edward was very dear to her. He could do no wrong. In her eyes, Angela was a thoroughly wicked woman, and Edward was well rid of her. But would any of her family find married happiness? Would poor Joan? Sometimes she began to doubt it, and looked back upon her own long years with Bender as something rare and strange.

Edward was at the wedding to give the bride

away. He looked thinner and older, and to Joan's way of thinking, handsomer than ever. He refused to speak of his own affairs, and set himself out to make Joan's wedding day the happiest one of her life.

With the exception of Sep and Robert the rest of Joan's relations were there with Kathy's auburn-haired daughter as bridesmaid, and Bertie and Kathy's small son as an inattentive page. Michael's mother was too ill to travel and his father too was absent, but a sister and brother, with the same devastating Irish good looks as the bridegroom, were present, and impressed old Mrs North very much by their piety in church.

'I must say,' she said to Winnie, in tones far too audible for her daughter's comfort, 'the Catholics do know how to behave in church. Not afraid to bend the knee when called for!'

Winnie was glad that something pleased the old lady, for she knew that she found the small church woefully lacking in amenities compared with Caxley's noble parish church built and made beautiful with the proceeds of the wool trade, so many centuries earlier.

There were few Roman Catholics in Caxley. One or two families from the marsh, descended from Irish labourers who had built the local railway line attended the church. Two ancient landed families came in each Sunday from the countryside south of the town, but there was little money to make the church beautiful. To old Mrs North the depressing green paint, the dingy pews and, above all, the crucified figure of Christ stretched bleeding high above the nave, were wholly distasteful. A church, she thought, should be a dignified and beautiful place, a true house of God, and a proper setting for the three great dramas of one's life, one's christening, one's marriage and one's funeral. This poor substitute was just not good enough, she decided firmly, as they waited for the bride.

Her eyes rested meditatively upon the bridegroom and his brother, and her heart, old but still susceptible, warmed suddenly. No doubt about it, they were a fine-looking family. One could quite see the attraction.

There was a flurry at the end of the church and the bride came slowly down the aisle on her brother's arm. Old Mrs North struggled to her feet, and looking at her granddaughter's radiant face, forgot her fears. If she knew anything about anything, this was one marriage in the Howard family which would turn out well!

## VICTORY

The honeymoon was spent at Burford and the sun shone for them. The old town had never looked lovelier, Joan thought, for she had visited it often before the war. This was Michael's first glimpse of the Cotswolds. He could not have seen Burford at a better time. The trees lining the steep High Street were in young leaf. The cottage gardens nodded with daffodils, and aubrietia and arabis hung their bright carpets over the grey stone walls.

As May broke, they returned to Caxley and to neglected news of the world of War. Much had happened. A photograph of the ghastly end of Mussolini and his mistress, Signorina Petacci, shocked them as it had shocked the world. And now, the suicide of Hitler was announced. On the last day of April, as Joan and Michael had wandered along the river bank at Burford, Hitler and his newly-married wife, Eva Braun had done themselves to death, with pistol and poison.

A week later came the unconditional surrender of the enemy. By that time, Michael was back with his regiment, and Joan watched the celebrations of victory with her family in the market square.

The cross of St George fluttered on the flag pole of St Peter's, close by the flapping Union Jack at the Town Hall. The Corn Exchange was draped with bunting and some irreverent reveller had propped a flag in Queen Victoria's hand. The public houses were busy, sounds of singing were abroad and everywhere people stopped to congratulate each other and share their relief.

But there was still the knowledge that the war was not completely finished, and Joan listened with her family to the voice of Churchill giving the nation grave thoughts in the midst of rejoicing.

'I wish,' he said, 'I could tell you tonight that all our toils and troubles were over. But, on the contrary, I must warn you that there is still a lot to do, and that you must be prepared for further efforts of mind and body.' He went on to point out that 'Beyond all lurks Japan, harassed and failing, but still a people of a hundred millions, for whose warriors death has few terrors.'

He was listened to with attention; but the moment was too happy to darken with sober warnings. For most of his hearers one splendid fact dazzled them. Victory in Europe was accomplished. Victory in the rest of the world must follow soon. And then, after six bloody years, they would have peace at last.

In the months that followed, old Mrs North spoke joyfully of returning to Rose Lodge. Winnie had her doubts about the wisdom of this step. Now that there were only the two of them to consider, the house seemed over-large, and they must face the problem of little or no help in running it. Mrs North refused to be persuaded.

'I absolutely set my face against finding another place,' she declared flatly. 'Rose Lodge is my home, bought for me by your dear father. The nurses are moving out in a month or two. There's no reason at all why we shouldn't get out the old furniture from store and move in right away. Besides, Edward will want this flat again the minute he's demobbed. We must leave everything ready for him.'

Winnie was wise enough to drop the subject for the time being, but returned to the attack whenever she had a chance. It was no use. The old lady was unshakeable in her determination.

'Go back,' Bertie advised his sister. 'Dash it all, she's getting on for eighty! She may as well enjoy her own for the rest of her time. Rose Lodge was all she ever wanted when she lived in the market place, and she's had to do without it for years.'

'I suppose we must,' sighed Winnie. 'But I shall shut off some of the rooms. It's a house that eats fuel, as you know, I really don't think I can cope with the cleaning singlehanded.

'We're all getting old,' agreed Bertie cheerfully. 'But I bet Mamma will be in and out of the locked rooms smartly enough with a duster.'

Soon after this Edward had a few days' leave, and within twenty-four hours was thanking his stars that his stay would be a short one. If anyone had ever told him that Caxley would pall, he would have denied it stoutly. But it was so.

He knew that he was under strain. He knew that Angela's desertion was a greater shock than he cared to admit. He was torn with remorse, with guilt, with what he might have left undone. He had thrown himself, with even more concentration, into his flying duties and now lived on the station, hoping, in part, to forget his trouble. All this added to the tension.

Perhaps he had relied too much on the healing powers of his native town. Perhaps, after all, he had outgrown the childhood instinct to return home when hurt. Perhaps the people of Caxley, his own family included, were as spent as he was after six years of lean times and anxiety. Whatever the causes, the results for Edward were plain. He could not return to Caxley to live, as things were.

His womenfolk said very little to him, but there was a false brightness in their tones when they did, and a sad brooding look of inner pain when they watched him. Edward found both unendurable. Bertie was the only person he could talk to, and to him he unburdened his heart.

'I just can't face it,' he said savagely, kicking the gravel on Bertie's garden path. 'Anyone'd think I was suddenly an idiot. They talk to me as though I'm a child who is ill. And then I snap at them, and feel an utter heel. God, what's going to be the end of it?'

'It's the hardest thing in the world,' observed Bertie, 'to accept pity gracefully. It's easy enough to give it.'

'It isn't only pity,' retorted Edward. 'There were two old cats whispering behind their hands in the restaurant, and I've had one or two pretty unpleasant remarks chucked at me. The top and bottom of it is that Caxley's little and mean, and I never saw it before. I feel stifled here – as though everyone has known and watched the Howards for generations. We're simply actors to them – people to look at, people to feed their own cheap desire for a bit of drama.'

'If you haven't realized that until now,' said Bertie calmly, 'you're a good deal more naïve than I thought. We all have to take our turn at being a nine days' wonder. It's yours now, and damned unpleasant too – but you'll be forgotten by next week when someone else crops up for the place in the limelight.'

'You're right,' agreed Edward bitterly. 'But it makes no difference to me for good, even if other people forget in a day or two. In any case I shall get a job elsewhere for a year or two, and then see how I feel about Caxley. What is there to bring me back?'

'Nothing,' said Bertie. 'Except us. I'm not trying to wring your withers and all that – but when this has blown over, I hope you'll want to come back to the family again.'

'Maybe I will. Maybe I won't. All I need now is to thrash about a bit and see other places and find a useful job. One thing, I'm alone now, and I'll take good care I stay that way. I've had enough of women's ways to last me a lifetime.'

Bertie observed his nephew's devastating, if

sulky, good looks with a quizzical eye, but forbore to comment on his last remark.

'There's a chap in the mess at the moment,' continued Edward, 'whose father runs a factory for making plastic things – a sort of progression from perspex and that type of thing. He says there should be a great future in plastic materials. Might even make them strong enough for use in building and ships and so on.'

'Would you want to go in for that sort of thing?'

'I'm interested,' nodded Edward. 'Jim took me to meet the old boy a few weeks ago. I liked him. He's got ideas and he works hard. I know he wants to build up the works as soon as he can. If he offered me a job, I think I'd take it.'

'Where would it be?'

'Near Ruislip. I'd rather like to be near London, too.'

'It sounds a good idea,' agreed Bertie, glad to see that his companion could still be kindled into life. 'I hope it comes off.'

They wandered through the garden gate to the towpath. The Cax reflected the blue and white sky above it. In the distance a fisherman sat immobile upon the opposite bank. Edward looked upon the tranquil scene with dislike, and skimmed a pebble viciously across the surface of the water towards the town.

'And at least I'd get away from here,' was his final comment.

The Cax flowed on placidly. It had seen centuries of men's tantrums. One more made very little difference.

That evening the occupants of the flat above Howard's Restaurant descended for their dinner. They did this occasionally when the restaurant was shut, and Robert was agreeable. He waited on them himself and joined the family party at coffee afterwards.

Sep came across and Bertie too was present. It was a cheerful gathering. Although the curtains were drawn across the windows looking on to the market place, those at the back of the building remained pulled back, and the sky still glowed with the remains of a fine July sunset. The little white tables and chairs, set out upon the grassy lawn sloping down gently to the Cax, glimmered in the twilight. It was comfortably familiar to Edward, and even his frayed nerves were soothed by the view which had remained the same now for years.

It was Joan who brought up the subject of Edward's return to the flat.

'How soon, do you think,' she asked, 'before you can come home again?'

Better now than later, decided Edward.

'I don't think that I shall come back to Caxley for a while,' he answered deliberately.

'Why ever not?' exclaimed old Mrs North. 'It's your home, isn't it?'

Edward drew a crescent very carefully on the white tablecloth with the edge of a spoon, and was silent.

'Edward's quite old enough to do as he pleases, Mamma,' said Bertie quietly.

'I hope you will come back, dear boy,' said Sep, putting a frail old hand on his grandson's sleeve.

'One day, perhaps,' said Edward, putting his own hand upon his grandfather's. 'But I want to have a spell elsewhere. You understand?'

'I understand,' said the old man gravely. 'You know what is best for you.'

'There's no need to feel that you are pushing us out,' began his mother, not quite understanding the situation. 'You know that we shall go back to Rose Lodge very soon.'

'Yes, dear, I do know that,' replied Edward, as patiently as he could. He drew a circle round the crescent, turning the whole into a plump face with a large mouth. He became conscious of Robert's eyes fixed upon him, and put down the spoon hastily, like a child caught out in some misdemeanour. But it was not the mutilation of the white starched surface which gave Robert that intent look, as Edward was soon to discover.

It was now almost dark and Sep rose to go, pleading a slight headache.

'I shall see you again before you leave,' he said to Edward, turning at the door. Edward watched him cross the market square, his heart full of affection for the small figure treading its familiar way homeward.

The ladies too had decided to retire. Goodnights were said, and Bertie, Edward and Robert were alone at the table. Robert carefully refilled the three coffee cups. His face was thoughtful.

'Have you any idea,' he asked 'when you'll come back to Caxley?'

'None,' said Edward shortly. 'At the moment I feel as though I want to turn my back on it for good.'

A sudden glint came into Robert's eyes. It was not unnoticed by the watchful Bertie.

'In that case,' said Robert swiftly, 'you won't want the rooms upstairs. Would you think of letting me have them? I would give you a good price to buy the whole of this property outright.'

Edward looked at Robert in astonishment. His Uncle Bertie's face had grown pink with concern.

'Thanks for the offer,' said Edward shortly, 'but I wouldn't do anything to upset Grandpa Howard. And in any case, I don't intend to part with the property.'

'You've no business to make such a suggestion,' exclaimed Bertie. His blue eyes flashed with unaccustomed fire. Edward had never seen his uncle so angry, and a very intimidating sight he found it.

'If he doesn't want it, why hang on to it?' demanded Robert. A little nerve twitched at the corner of his mouth, and he glared across the table at his brother-in-law.

'He may want it one day,' pointed out Bertie, 'as well you know. It is unfair to take advantage of the boy at a time like this. More than unfair – it's outrageous!'

'He's being nothing more nor less than a dog in the manger,' retorted Robert heatedly. 'He doesn't want it, but he'll dam' well see I don't have it! Why on earth the old man ever made such a barmy arrangement I shall never know! I'm his son, aren't I? How does he expect me to run this place with no storage rooms above it? The old fool gets nearer his dotage daily – and others profit by it!'

Edward, who had grown tired of listening to the two men arguing his affairs as though he were not present, felt that he could stand no more.

'Oh, shut up, both of you,' he cried. 'We'll keep Grandpa out of this, if you don't mind. And forget the whole thing. You can take it from me, Robert, the house remains mine as he intended, whether I live here or not, and you must like it or lump it.'

He rose from the table, looking suddenly intensely weary.

'I'm off to bed. See you in the morning. Goodnight!'

'I'm off too,' said Bertie grimly. He limped towards the door of the restaurant as Edward began to mount the stairs to his own apartment.

He heard the door crash behind his uncle, and then two sounds, like pistol shots, as Robert viciously slammed the bolts home.

The sooner I get out of this, the better, determined Edward, taking the last flight of stairs two at a time.

The next morning he made his round of farewells cheerfully. Robert seemed to have forgotten the previous evening's unpleasantness and wished him well. Sep's handshake was as loving as ever. He called last of all on Bertie.

'I'm sorry I lost my temper last night,' Bertie greeted him. 'I hate to say this, Edward, but you must be wary of Robert. He's a man with a grievance, and to my mind he gets odder as the years go by.'

'I'll watch out,' smiled Edward, making light of it.

'He's let this separation of the house and the restaurant become an obsession,' continued Bertie, 'and he's decidedly unbalanced when the subject crops up. Hang on to your own, my boy. It would break Sep's heart if he thought you'd broken with Caxley for good.'

'I know that,' said Edward quietly.

They parted amicably, glad to know each other's feelings, and Edward made his way up Caxley High Street noticing the placards on the buildings and in shop windows exhorting the good people of Caxley to support rival candidates in the coming election. Not that there would be much of a fight in this secure Conservative seat, thought Edward. The outcome was a foregone conclusion. And so, he felt sure, was the return of the Conservative party to power. The hero of the hour was Winston Churchill. It was unthinkable that he should not lead the nation in peacetime, and as bravely as he had in these last five years of grim warfare.

He was right about Caxley's decision. The Conservative candidate was returned, but by a majority so small that his supporters were considerably shaken. When at last the nation's wishes were made known, and the Socialists were returned with a large majority, Edward was flabbergasted and disgusted, and said so in the mess.

Back in Caxley old Mrs North summed up the feelings of many of her compatriots, as she studied the newspaper on the morning of 27 July.

'To think that dear Mr Churchill has got to go after all he's done for the nation! The ungrateful lot! I'm thoroughly ashamed of them. The poor man will take this very hard, and you can't wonder at it, can you? I shall sit straight down, Winnie dear, and write to him.'

And, with back straight as a ramrod and blue eyes afire, she did.

The end of the conflict was now very close. Millions of leaflets demanding surrender were showered on the inhabitants of Japan. The last warning of 'complete and utter destruction' was given on 5 August. On the following day the first atomic bomb was cast upon Hiroshima, and on 9 August a second one was dropped on the city of Nagasaki. Within a week the terms set out by the Allied governments were accepted, and the new Prime Minister, Mr Attlee, broadcast the news at midnight.

Overwhelming relief was, of course, the first reaction. There were still a few places in the Far East where fighting continued, but virtually this was the end of the war. Soon the men would be back, and life would return to normal.

Sep surveyed the happy crowds from his bedroom window, and thought of that other victory, nearly thirty years earlier, when the flags had fluttered and the people of Caxley had greeted peace with a frenzy of rejoicing. Today there was less madness, less hysteria. It had been a long bitter struggle, and there had been many casualties, but the numbers had been less than in that earlier cruel war.

He remembered how he had stood grieving for his dead son amidst his neighbours' cheers. Thank God that his family had been spared this time! He looked down upon the bronze crown of Queen Victoria below him, and wondered inconsequently what she would make of a victory finally won by an atomic bomb. The descriptions of its ghastly power had affected Sep deeply.

Now that such forces were known to the world, what did the future hold for mankind? What if such a weapon fell into the hands of a maniac like Hitler? Would the world ever be safe again?

Four young men, aflame with bonhomie and beer, had caught each other by the coat tails and were stamping round Queen Victoria's plinth shouting rhythmically 'Victory for us! Victory for us! Victory for us!' to the delight of the crowd.

Sep turned sadly from the window. Victory indeed, but at what a price, mourned the old man, at what a price!

# Part Two
# 1945–1950

### EDWARD STARTS AFRESH

The return to Rose Lodge was accompanied by the usual frustrations and set-backs. The decorators waited for the plasterers' work to be completed. The electricians waited for the plumbers to finish their part. A chimney was faulty. Damp patches had appeared mysteriously on the landing ceiling. The paintwork inside and out showed the neglect of six years of war and hard wear.

At times Winnie wished that she had stuck to her guns and refused point blank to return. But her mother's joy was not a whit dampened by the delays, and she threw herself with zest into the job of choosing wallpaper and curtaining from the meagre stocks available. Tirelessly she searched the shops for all the odds and ends needed to refurbish her home. One morning she would be matching fringe for the curtains, or gimp for a newly upholstered chair; on the next she would be comparing prices of coke and anthracite for the kitchen boiler. She was just as busy and excited as she had been years ago, Winnie recalled, when the family moved to Rose Lodge for the first time. Bertie had been quite right. Rose Lodge meant everything to their mother, and it was obviously best that she should spend the rest of her days there.

They moved from the market square on a blustery November day. Ragged low clouds raced across the sky. The Caxley folk, cowering beneath shuddering umbrellas, battled against the wind that buffeted them. Vicious showers of rain slanted across the streets, and the removal men dripped rivulets from their shiny macintoshes as they heaved the furniture down the stairs and into the van.

But, by the evening, Winnie and her mother sat exhausted but triumphant one on each side of the familiar drawing-room hearth.

'Home, at last,' sighed the old lady happily, looking about her. It was still far from perfect. The curtains hung stiffly, the carpet had some extraordinary billows in it, the removal men had scraped the paint by the door and chipped a corner of the china cabinet, but she was content.

'And to think,' she continued, 'that Edward will be demobilized in a few weeks' time, and dear Bertie, and perhaps Michael, and we can all have a proper family Christmas here together. The first peacetime Christmas!'

'I wonder how Joan's managing,' answered

Winnie, still bemused from the day's happenings. 'I hope she won't feel lonely.'

'Lonely?' echoed her mother, 'In the market place? Take my word for it, she's as right as ninepence with the flat to play with and her own nice new things to arrange. She'll thoroughly enjoy having a place of her own.'

'You're probably right, Mamma,' said Winnie. 'Early bed for us tonight. There are muscles aching in my back and arms which I never knew I had before.'

By ten o'clock Rose Lodge was in darkness and its two occupants slept the sleep of the happy and exhausted.

It was Joan who had written to Edward to ask if she and Michael might have the flat temporarily, and he was delighted to think of it being of use to the young couple. He had been offered a good post in the plastics firm, as he had hoped, and was already looking forward to finding a flat or a house somewhere near London and the job.

This suited Joan and Michael admirably. It was plain that the nursery school would close now that the war was over, despite the recommendations of the Education Act of 1944. Joan grieved at the thought, but numbers were dwindling steadily, as the men came back, and the evacuees moved away from Caxley. By Easter the school would be no more, and the Quaker meeting house which had echoed to the cries and mirth of the babies, tumbling about the scrubbed floor in their blue-checked overalls, would once more be silent and empty, but for the decorous meetings of the children's war-time hosts, the Friends.

She was glad, though, that she had a job to do, for it transpired that Michael's demobilization would be deferred. He was now in Berlin, and his fluency in German was of great use. He had been given further promotion and been asked to stay on until the spring, but he had Christmas leave and the two spent a wonderful week arranging their wedding presents and buying furniture for the future.

'None of this blasted utility stuff,' declared Michael flatly. 'I'm sick of that sign anyway. We'll pick up second-hand pieces as we go – things we shall always like.' And so they went to two sales, and haunted the furniture shops in Caxley High Street which offered the old with the new.

Christmas Day was spent at Rose Lodge to please Mrs North. Edward and Bertie, recently demobilized, were in high spirits. All the conversation was of the future and Winnie, surveying the Norths and Howards filling the great drawing-room, thought how right it was that it should be so. The immediate past was bleak and tragic; and, for her particularly, earlier years in this house held sad memories. She remembered arriving with Joan as a baby and Edward as a toddler to find her mother dressing the Christmas tree in just the same place as the present one. Leslie had left her, and the long lonely years had just begun. She often wondered what had become of him – the handsome charmer whose son was so shatteringly like him in looks – but hoped never to see him again. He had hurt her too cruelly.

One evening before Michael returned to Germany, Joan and he talked over their plans for the future. At one time he had thought of following up his Dublin degree with a year's training for his teacher's diploma, but now he had his doubts about this course.

'I don't think I could face sitting at a desk and poring over books again. The war's unsettled me – I want to start doing something more practical. I've talked to other fellows who broke their university course, or who had just finished, like me, and there are mighty few who have got the guts to return to the academic grind again. Somehow one's brain gets jerked out of the learning groove. I know for a fact mine has.'

He faced Joan with a smile.

'Besides,' he continued, 'I've a wife and a future family to support now. I must earn some money to keep the home together. We shan't want to stay in Caxley all our lives, you know, and we shall have to buy a house before long.'

'But what do you want to do?' asked his wife earnestly. 'I do understand about not wanting to go back to school, I couldn't face it myself. But what else have you thought of? It seems a pity not to use your languages.'

'I wouldn't mind doing the same sort of thing that my father does – hotel work. Here or abroad. I'm easy. And perhaps, one day, owning our own hotel. Or a chain of them.'

His eyes were sparkling. He spoke lightly, but Joan could see that there was an element of serious purpose behind the words.

'Or I could stay in the army. That's been put to me. What do you feel about that, my sweet?'

'Horrible,' said Joan flatly. 'I've had enough of the army; and the idea of moving from one army camp to another doesn't appeal to me one little bit. And you know how *backward* army children are, poor dears, shunted from pillar to post and just getting the hang of one reading method when they're faced with an entirely different one.'

Michael laughed at this practical teacher's approach.

'I can't say I'm keen to stay myself,' he agreed. 'Six years is enough for me. We'd be better off, of course, but is it worth it?'

'Never,' declared Joan stoutly. 'Let's be poor and lead our own lives.'

And with that brave dictum they shelved the future for the remainder of his leave.

Meanwhile, Edward had been finding out just

how difficult it was to get somewhere to live near London. He tried two sets of digs whilst he was flat hunting and swore that he would never entertain the thought of lodgings again. The only possible hotel within striking distance of the factory was expensive, noisy, and decidedly seedy.

It was Jim, the son of his employer, who saved him at last.

'I've got a house,' he cried triumphantly one morning, bursting into the office which he shared with Edward. 'It's scruffy, it's jerry-built, but it's got three bedrooms and a garden. Eileen is off her head with delight. Now the boy can have a bedroom of his own, and the baby too when it arrives.'

Edward congratulated him warmly. Then a thought struck him.

'And what about the flat?'

'A queue for that as long as your arm,' began Jim. He stopped pacing the floor and looked suddenly at his colleague. 'Want it?' he asked, 'because if you do, it could be yours. The others can wait. I'll have a word with the old man.'

After a little negotiation, it was arranged, and Edward moved in one blue and white March day. A speculative builder, an old school friend of Edward's employer, had acquired the site a few years before the war, and had erected two pairs of presumably semi-detached houses, well placed in one large garden. Each house was divided into two self-contained flats, so that there were eight households all told in about an acre of ground.

The plot was situated at the side of an old tree-lined lane and was not far from a golf course. A cluster of fir trees and a mature high hedge screened the flats from the view of passers-by. The ground-floor tenants agreed to keep the front part of the garden in order, the upstairs tenants the back.

The rent was pretty steep, Edward privately considered, by Caxley standards, but he liked the flat and its secluded position and would have paid even more for the chance of escaping from digs and hotels. He surveyed his new domain thankfully. He had a sitting-room, one bedroom, a kitchen, a bathroom and a gloriously large cupboard for trunks, tennis racquets, picnic baskets and all the other awkward objects which need to be housed. He was well content.

He saw little of his neighbours in the first few weeks, and learned more about them from Jim than from his own brief encounters. His own flat was on the ground-floor, and immediately beside him lived a middle-aged couple, distantly related to the owner, and now retired. Edward liked the look of them. The wife had wished him 'Good morning' in a brisk Scots brogue and her husband reminded him slightly of his grandfather, Bender North.

Above them lived a sensible-looking woman, a little older than Edward himself, who mounted a spruce bicycle each morning and pedalled energetically away. Edward had decided that she was an efficient secretary in one of the nearby factories, but Jim told him otherwise.

'Headmistress of an infants' school,' he informed him. 'Miss Hedges – a nice old bird. She was awfully kind to Eileen when she was having our first. And the two above you are secretaries, or so they say. I'd put them as shorthand-typists myself, but no doubt they'll rise in the scale before very long. Flighty, but harmless, you'll find.'

'And decorative,' added Edward. 'And much addicted to bathing. One at night and one in the morning, I've worked out. There's a cascade by my ear soon after eleven and another just after seven each morning, down the waste pipe.'

'Come to think of it,' said Jim, 'I believe you're right. Trust a countryman to find out all the details of his neighbours' affairs! It had never occurred to me, I must admit.'

'It's a pity my grandmother can't spend an afternoon there,' replied Edward. 'She'd have the life history of every one of us at her finger tips before the sun set! Now, Jim, let's get down to work.'

The first Caxley visitors to the flat were his Uncle Bertie and Aunt Kathy, on their way to meet friends in London.

'You look so happy!' exclaimed his aunt, kissing him. She stood back and surveyed him with her sparkling dark eyes. 'And so smart!' she added.

'My demob suit,' said Edward, with a grimace. 'And tie, too.'

'Well, at least the tie's wearable,' observed Bertie. 'At the end of my war, I was offered the choice of a hideous tie or "a very nice neckerchief". How d'you like that?'

Edward pressed them for all the Caxley news. Bertie noticed that he was eager for every detail of the family. How soon, he wondered, before he would return? Certainly, he had visited Rose Lodge on several occasions, and his present home was conveniently near Western Avenue for him to make his way to Caxley within a short time. At the moment, however, it looked as though Edward was comfortably settled. His decree nisi was already through; before the end of the year he should be free, but as things were, it seemed pretty plain that his nephew was happy to return to a bachelor's existence.

The greatest piece of news they had to offer was that Joan was expecting a child in the late summer, and that Michael, now demobilized, had decided to learn more about the catering trade by working for a time in Howard's Restaurant. Sep had suggested this move, and although Michael realized that there might be difficulties, he was glad to accept the work as a temporary measure, until the baby arrived.

'And how has Robert taken it?' asked Edward,

after expressing his delight at the prospect of becoming an uncle.

'Fairly quietly, so far. I don't think it would be very satisfactory permanently though. His temper is getting more and more unpredictable. Two waitresses have left in the last month. It's my belief he's ill, but he flatly refuses to see the doctor.'

'He's a queer customer,' agreed Edward, 'but times are difficult. He must have a devil of a job getting supplies. Food seems to be shorter now than during the war – unless it's because I'm a stranger here and don't get anything tucked away under the counter for me. I'd starve if it weren't for the works' canteen midday, and some of the stuff they dish up there is enough to make you shudder.'

'Father says that people mind most about bread rationing,' said Kathy. ' "Never had it in our lives before," they said, really shocked, you know. And poor dear, he *will* get all these wretched bits of paper, bread units, *absolutely* right. You know what a stickler he is. I was in the shop the other day helping him. People leave their pages with him and then have a regular order for a cake, using so many each week. It makes an enormous amount of book work for the poor old darling. Sometimes I try to persuade him to give up. He's practically eighty, after all.'

'He won't,' commented Bertie, 'he'll die in harness, and like it that way. And Robert's more of a liability than a help at the moment. He resents the fact that Sep didn't hand over the business to him outright, when he gave you the house. It's beginning to become more of an obsession than ever, I'm afraid.'

'He was always dam' awkward about that,' said Edward shortly. 'Good heavens! Surely Grandpa can do as he likes with his own? If there's anything I detest it's this waiting for other men's shoes – like a vulture.'

'Vultures don't wear shoes,' pointed out Kathy, surveying her own neat pair. 'And whatever it is that screws up our poor Robert it makes things downright unpleasant for us all, particularly Father.'

'And Michael and Joan?'

'Michael's such a good-tempered fellow,' said Bertie, 'that he'll stand a lot. And Joan's at the blissfully broody stage just now. I caught her winding wool with Maisie Hunter the other evening with a positively maudlin expression on her face.'

'Maisie Hunter?' echoed Edward. 'I thought she'd got married.'

'Her husband-to-be crashed on landing at Brize Norton, about six weeks before the war ended.'

'I never heard that,' Edward said slowly. 'Poor Maisie.'

Bertie glanced at his watch and rose to go.

'Come along, my dear,' he said, hauling Kathy

to her feet. 'We shall meet all the homegoing traffic, if we don't look out.'

Edward accompanied them to the gate and waved good-bye as the car rounded the bend in the lane. It was strange, he thought, how little he envied them returning to Caxley. It was another world, and one which held no attraction for him. Much as he loved his family, he was glad that he was free of the tensions and squabbles in which they seemed now involved.

He bent down to pull a few weeds from the garden bed which bordered the path, musing the while on his change of outlook. He revelled in his present anonymous role. It was wonderful to know that one's neighbours took so little interest in one's affairs. It was refreshing to be able to shut the door and be absolutely unmolested in the flat, to eat alone, to sleep alone, and to be happy or sad as the spirit moved one, without involving other people's feelings. It was purely selfish, of course, he knew that, but it was exactly what he needed.

He straightened his aching back and looked aloft. An aeroplane had taken off from nearby Northolt aerodrome and he felt the old rush of pleasure in its soaring power. And yet, here again, there was a difference. He felt not the slightest desire to fly now. Would the longing ever return? Or would this numb apathy which affected him remain always with him, dulling pleasure and nullifying pain?

It was useless to try to answer these questions. He must be thankful for the interest of the new job, and for this present quietness in which to lick his wounds. Perhaps happiness and warmth, ambition and purpose, would return to him one day. Meanwhile, he must try and believe all the tiresome people who kept reminding him that 'Time was the Great Healer'.

Perhaps, they might, just possibly, be right.

## A FAMILY TRAGEDY

As the summer advanced, affairs in the market place went from bad to worse. The aftermath of the war – general fatigue – was felt everywhere. Food was not the only thing in short supply. Men returning from active service found it desperately hard to find somewhere to live. Women, longing for new clothes, for colour, for gaiety, still had to give coupons for garments and for material for making them, as well as for all the soft furnishings needed. 'Makes you wonder who won the war!' observed someone bitterly, watching Sep clip out the precious snippets of paper entitling her to three loaves, and the feeling was everywhere.

Sep, hard-pressed with work and smaller than ever in old age, maintained his high standards of service steadily. But he was a worried man. The shop was doing as well as ever, but the returns from the restaurant showed a slight decline as the weeks went by, and Sep knew quite well that Robert was at fault. It was becoming more and more difficult to keep staff. Robert was short with the waitresses in front of customers, and impatient and sarcastic with the kitchen staff. How long, wondered Sep, before Michael, who was working so wonderfully well, found conditions unendurable?

He made up his mind to take Robert aside privately and have a talk with him. The fellow was touchy and might sulk, as he had so often done as a boy, but at the rate he was going on Howard's Restaurant would soon be in Queer Street. Sep did not relish the task, but he had never shirked his duty in his life, and it was plain that this unpleasant encounter must take place.

He crossed the square from the shop as the Town Hall clock struck eight. The restaurant was closed, the staff had gone and Robert was alone in the kitchen reading *The Caxley Chronicle*. Sep sat down opposite him.

'My boy, I'll come straight to the point. Business is slipping, as you know. Any particular reason?'

'Only that I'm expected to run this place with a set of fools,' muttered Robert, scowling at his clenched hands on the table top.

'I'm worried more about you than the business,' said Sep gently. 'You've been overdoing it. Why not take a holiday? We could manage, you know, for a week, say.'

Robert jumped to his feet, his face flushing.

'And let Michael worm his way in? Is that what you want? It's to be Edward all over again, I can see. What's wrong with me – your own son – that you should slight me all the time?'

'My boy –' began Sep, protesting, but he was overwhelmed by Robert's passionate outburst.

'What chance have I ever had? Edward has the house given him at twenty-one. The house that should have been mine anyway. Do I get given anything? Oh no! I can wait – wait till I'm old and useless, with nothing to call my own.'

His face was dark and congested, the words spluttered from his mouth. To Sep's horror he saw tears welling in his son's eyes and trickling down his cheeks. The pent-up resentment of years was bursting forth and Sep could do nothing to quell the violence.

'I've never had a fair deal from the day I was born. Jim was a hero because he got himself killed. No one was ever allowed to mention Leslie, though he was the kindest of the lot to me, and I missed him more than any of you. Kath's been the spoilt baby all her life, and I've been general dog's body. Work's all I've ever had, with no time for anything else. The rest of the family have homes and children. I've been too busy for girls. Edward and Bertie and Michael came back from the war jingling with medals. What did I get for sticking here as a slave? I'm despised, I tell you! Despised! Laughed at – by all Caxley –'

By now he was sobbing with self-pity, beating his palms against his forehead in a childish gesture which wrung his father's heart. Who would have dreamt that such hidden fires had smouldered for so long beneath that timid exterior? And what could be done to comfort him and to give him back pride in himself?

Sep let the storm subside a little before he spoke. His voice was gentle.

'I'm sorry that you should feel this way, my boy. You've let your mind dwell on all sorts of imagined slights. You were always as dear to me and your mother as the other children – more so, perhaps, as the youngest. No one blames you for not going to the war. You were rejected through no fault of your own. Everyone here knows that you've done your part by sticking to your job here.'

Robert's sobbing had ceased, but he scowled across the table mutinously.

'It's a lie! Everyone here hates me. People watch me wherever I go. They talk about me behind my back. I know, I tell you, I know! They say I couldn't get a girl if I tried. They say no one wants me. They say I'm under my dad's thumb – afraid to stand on my own feet – afraid to answer back! I'm a failure. That's what they say, watching and whispering about me, day in and day out!'

Sep stood up, small, straight and stern.

'Robert, you are over-wrought, and don't know what you are saying. But I won't hear you accusing innocent people of malice. All this is in your own mind. You must see this, surely?'

Robert approached his father. There was a strange light in his glittering eyes. He thrust his face very close to the old man's.

'My mind?' he echoed. 'Are you trying to say I'm out of my mind? I know well enough what people are saying about me. I hear them. But I hear other voices too – *private* voices that tell me I'm right, that the whisperers in Caxley will be confounded, and that the time will come when they have to give in and admit that Robert Howard was right all the time. They'll see me one day, the owner of this business here, the owner of the shop, the biggest man in the market square, the head of the Howard family!'

His voice had risen with excitement, his eyes were wild. From weeping self-pity he had swung in the space of minutes to a state of manic euphoria. He began to pace the floor, head up, nostrils flaring, as he gulped for breath.

'You'll be gone by then,' he cried triumphantly, 'and I'll see that Edward goes too. There will be one Howard only in charge. Just one. One to give orders. One to be the boss!'

'Robert!' thundered Sep, in the voice which he had used but rarely in his life. There was no response. Robert was in another world, oblivious of his father and his surroundings.

'They'll see,' he continued, pacing even more swiftly. 'My time will come. My voices know. They tell me the truth. "The persecutors shall become the persecuted!" That's what my voices tell me.'

Sep walked round the table and confronted his son. He took hold of his elbows and looked steadily into that distorted face a little above his own.

'Robert,' he said clearly, as though to a distraught child. 'We are going home now, and you are going to bed.'

The young man's gaze began to soften. His eyes turned slowly towards his father's. He looked as though he were returning from a long, strange journey.

'Very well, father,' he said. The voice was exhausted, but held a certain odd pride, as though remnants of glimpsed grandeur still clung to him.

He watched his father lock up. Sep, white-faced and silent, walked beside his son across the market square, watching him anxiously.

Robert, head high, looked to the left and right as he strode proudly over the cobbles. He might have been a king acknowledging the homage of his people, except that, to Sep's relief, the square was empty. When they reached their door

Robert entered first, as of right, and swept regally up the stairs to his room, without a word.

When faithful old Miss Taggerty brought in Sep's bed-time milk, she found her master sitting pale and motionless.

'You don't look yourself, sir,' she said with concern. 'Shall I bring you anything? An aspirin, perhaps?'

'I'm all right. Just a little tired.'

'Shall I fetch Mr Robert?'

'No, no! Don't worry about me. I'm off to bed immediately.'

They wished each other good night. Sep watched the door close quietly behind the good-hearted creature, and resumed his ponderings.

What was to be done? Tonight had made plain something which he had long suspected. Robert's mind was giving way under inner torment. He was obsessed with a wrongful sense of grievance against himself, and worse still, a gnawing jealousy, aimed chiefly against Edward. These two evils had become his masters. There were 'the voices' which he claimed to hear, and which were driving him beyond the brink of sanity.

To Sep's generation, insanity in the family was something to be kept from the knowledge of outsiders. One pitied the afflicted, but one kept the matter as quiet as possible. So often, he knew from experience, attacks passed and, within a few months, rest and perhaps a change of scene, brought mental health again. It might be so with Robert.

He disliked the idea of calling in a doctor to the boy. Suppose that Robert were sent to a mental home? Would he ever come out again? Did doctors really know what went on in the human brain, and could they cure 'a mind diseased'? Wouldn't the mere fact of consulting a doctor upset his poor son's condition even more?

And yet the boy was in need of help, and he was the last person to be able to give it. How terrible it had been to hear that awful indictment of himself as a father! Was he really to blame? Had he loved him less? In all humility he felt that he could truthfully claim to have loved all his children equally – even Leslie, who had betrayed him.

And those fearful indications of a deluded mind – the assumption of omnipotence, of grandeur, to what might they lead? Would he become violent if he were ridiculed in one of these moods? Sep remembered the menacing glitter in his son's eyes, and trembled for him. What did the future hold for Robert?

He took his milk with him to the bedroom. The blinds were drawn against the familiar view of the market square and the indomitable figure of Queen Victoria. Miss Taggerty had turned the bedclothes back into a neat white triangle. Sep knelt beside the bed and prayed for guidance.

When he arose his mind was clear. He would sleep on this problem and see how things fared in the morning. There was no need to rush for help to the rest of the family. This was something to be borne alone if possible, so that Robert should be spared further indignities. He had suffered enough, thought Sep, torn with pity.

For a few weeks things went more smoothly. Robert never referred to that dreadful outburst. It was as though it had been wiped completely from his memory. For Sep, the incident was unforgettable, but he said nothing.

Nevertheless, it was obvious that the young man was in a precarious state of mind. Sep did what he could to relieve the pressure of work at the restaurant, and Michael's efforts ensured the smooth running of the place. His cheerfulness and good looks soon made him popular, which was good for trade but not, as Sep realized, for Robert's esteem.

Kathy, knowing that staff were hard to get at the restaurant offered to help whenever possible. She and Bertie realized that Robert was under strain, although they had no idea of the seriousness of his malaise.

'You'd be more use, my dear, in the shop,' said Sep. 'It would leave me free to go across to Robert's more often, and you know exactly where everything is at home.'

'I was brought up to it,' laughed Kathy. 'I'd

enjoy it, you know, and now that the children are off my hands, it will give me an interest.'

Her presence was a great comfort to Sep, and meant that he could keep a discreet, if anxious, eye on affairs across the square.

During these uneasy weeks Joan's baby was born. It was a girl, and the family were all delighted. She was born in the nursing home to the north of Caxley, on the road to Beech Green and Fairacre, where so many other Caxley citizens had first seen the light. Michael was enormously pleased and visited his wife and daughter every evening.

Joan remained there for a fortnight. It was decided that she should go for a week or two to Rose Lodge to regain her strength, and submit to the welcome cossetings of her mother and grandmother. The house was certainly more convenient than the flat, and the baby would have the benefit of the garden air as well as the doting care of three women. She was to be christened Sarah.

'No hope of the poor little darling being christened at St Peter's, I suppose?' sighed Mrs North.

'You know there isn't,' replied Joan, smiling at her grandmother's naughtiness.

'I never seem to have any luck with family ceremonies,' commented the old lady. She brightened as a thought crossed her mind. 'Perhaps Kathy's girl one day?'

Soon after Joan returned to the flat trouble began again. Robert's antagonism towards Michael was renewed in a hundred minor insults. Despite his easy-going disposition, Michael's Irish blood was roused.

'The fellow's off his rocker,' declared Michael roundly one evening in the privacy of the flat. 'He's beginning to talk as though he's the King of England. Sometimes I wonder if we should stay.'

Letters from his family in Dublin had also unsettled him. His father was in failing health and it was plain that he longed for his son to return to carry on the hotel, although he did not press the boy to come if his prospects were brighter in Caxley. Joan did not know how to advise her husband. She herself half-feared the uprooting and the break with the family, especially with a young child to consider. On the other hand it was right that Michael should obey his conscience, and she would do whatever he felt was best. Certainly, as things were, there was nothing but petty frustrations for Michael in his work, and he had obviously learned all that could be learned from the comparatively small Caxley restaurant. It was time he took on something bigger, giving him scope for his ability.

She told her problem to her old friend Maisie Hunter, who was to be godmother to Sarah. Her answer was straightforward.

'Michael's trying to spare you. Tell him you'll

be happy to go to Dublin, and then watch his face. I'm sure he wants to go back home, and he's bound to do well.'

She was right, and the couple had almost decided to break the news to Sep and Robert and to write to Michael's father, when two things happened to clinch the matter.

Joan had put her daughter to sleep in the pram in the little garden sloping down to the Cax, when Robert burst from the restaurant in a state of fury.

'I won't have that thing out here,' he said, kicking at a wheel. 'This is part of my restaurant, as you well know. You can clear off!'

'Robert!' protested Joan, much shocked. 'I've always used the garden. What on earth has come over you?'

Two or three curious customers, taking morning coffee, gazed with interest upon the scene from the restaurant windows. Joan was horribly aware of their presence, and took Robert's arm to lead him further away. He flung her from him with such violence that she fell across the pram. The child broke into crying, and Joan, now thoroughly alarmed, lifted her from the pram.

'You'll use the garden no more,' shouted Robert. 'You're trespassing on my property. And if you leave that contraption here I shall throw it in the river!'

At this moment, Michael arrived, and took in the situation at a glance.

'Take the baby upstairs,' he said quietly. 'I'll deal with this.'

He propelled the struggling and protesting Robert into the little office at the end of the restaurant and slammed the door, much to the disappointment of the interested customers. He thrust Robert into an arm chair, and turned to get him a drink from the cupboard. He was white with fury, and his hand shook as he poured out a stiff tot, but he was in command of himself and the situation. He was facing an ill man, and a dangerous one, he realized.

Robert leapt from the chair, as Michael put the glass on the desk, and tried to make for the door. Michael administered a hard slap to each cheek, as one would to an hysterical patient, and Robert slumped again into the chair.

'Drink this slowly,' commanded Michael, 'and wait here until I get back.'

He left the office, turned the key in the lock, and told good old John Bush who had been in Sep's employ for forty years, to take charge while he saw to his wife and let Sep know what was happening.

Later that evening Sep, Bertie and Michael held counsel.

'We must get a doctor to see him,' said Bertie firmly. 'I'll ring Dr Rogers tonight.'

'I blame myself,' said Sep heavily. 'He has not been himself for months. We should have got help earlier. It must be done now. I fear for Joan and the child if he is going to get these attacks of violence.'

'I want them to go back to Rose Lodge, but Joan is very much against it,' said Michael. 'But it's going to be impossible to stay over the restaurant, if he doesn't change his ways.'

'Let's get the doctor's verdict before we do anything more,' said Bertie.

Dr Rogers said little when he had examined his patient, but his grave looks alarmed Sep.

'Will he get better?' he asked anxiously. 'He's such a young man – so many years before him. What do you think?'

Dr Rogers would not commit himself, but provided various bottles of pills and promised to visit frequently. Meanwhile, he asked the family to call him in immediately if the symptoms of excessive excitement occurred again.

A few days later a letter arrived from Ireland from Michael's invalid mother. His father was sinking. Could he return? And was there any hope of him taking over the hotel?

'This settles it,' said Joan, looking at Michael's worried face as he read the letter again.

'But what about Howard's Restaurant? How will Sep manage?'

'John Bush can run the place blindfold. And Aunt Kathy would help, I know. Go and tell Sep what has happened. Take the letter.'

She knew full well how Sep would react.

'Of course you must go, my boy. Your father

comes first, and your mother needs your presence at a time like this. You've been of enormous help to us here, but it's right that you should start a life of your own.'

And so, within two days, Michael returned to Dublin, and Joan and the baby were to join him as soon as possible. It was Bertie who drove them to Holyhead to catch the boat to Dun Laoghaire. Saying farewell to the family had been ineffably sad.

'I'll be back soon for a holiday,' she told them all bravely. It was hardest to say good-bye to Sep and Grandma North. They looked so old, so shattered at the parting.

'You are doing the right thing,' Sep assured her firmly. 'I'm sure you have a wonderful future in Ireland.'

Her grandmother was less hopeful and inclined to be tearful.

'Such a *long* way off, and a very wild sort of people, I hear. The thought of all those poor babies of yours being brought up in such *strange* ways quite upsets me. Do boil all the water, dear, whatever you do.'

Joan promised, and kissed her, hardly knowing whether to laugh or cry. Funny, exasperating, old Grandma! How long before she saw her again?

Dr Rogers' treatment seemed to have only a small sedative effect on Robert, but Sep tried to assure himself that the cure was bound to take a long time, and that his son's youth and a lessening of his work would finally ensure his recovery.

Kathy insisted on taking over the financial affairs of the restaurant while John Bush coped with the practical side. She was as quick at figures as her mother, Edna Howard, had been, and soon proved a competent business woman.

It was quite apparent that Robert resented her intrusion into his affairs, and Kathy ignored the snubs and sarcastic comments which punctuated the day's work. Robert was sick. Soon he would be better, and he would be happy again, she thought.

She was totally unprepared, therefore, for a sudden attack of the mania which had so appalled Sep months before. It happened, luckily, soon after the restaurant had closed and Kathy was checking the money. Perhaps the clinking of the coins reminded him of the fact that the business was not his. Perhaps the sight of his sister, sitting in the chair which had always been his own, inflamed him. No one would ever know; but resentment flared again, his voice grew loud and strident as he screamed his hatred of his family and his intention to get rid of them.

'My voices told me,' he roared at the terrified Kathy. 'They told me I would triumph, and I shall! Michael and Joan have gone. Old Bush will go, and you will go! There will be no one left but me – the unbeatable – the true heir!'

His lips were flecked with saliva, his eyes demented, as he bore down upon her. Dropping the money on the floor, Kathy tore open the door, and fled across the square to find help, the jingle of the rolling coins ringing in her ears.

The next day an ambulance took Robert and his attendants to the county mental hospital some twenty miles away. Sep, shattered, sat trying to understand Dr Rogers' explanation of his son's illness. He heard but one phrase in four and many of those were inexplicable to him. 'A progressively worsening condition,' he understood painfully well, but such terms as 'manic depressive' and the seriousness of 'hearing voices', as symptoms, meant nothing to the desolate old man.

To Sep, who knew his Bible, 'the voices' were simply Robert's demons – the outcome of the twin evils of jealousy and self-pity. Robert had been weak. He had succumbed to the temptations of his demons. His madness was, in part, a punishment for flying in the face of Providence.

When the doctor had gone, Sep stood at the back window and looked upon the row of willows lining the bank of the Cax. Three sons had once been his, gay little boys who had tumbled about the yard and moulded pastry in the bakehouse in their small fat hands.

One was long dead, one long-estranged, and now the last of the three was mad. Sep's life had been long and hard, but that moment by the window was the most desolate and despairing he had ever known.

## NEW HORIZONS

Edward heard the news about Robert in a letter from his mother. He was deeply shocked, and very anxious about the effect this blow might have on his grandfather. He was thankful to know that his Aunt Kathy and John Bush were coping so ably with the restaurant, and glad to give permission to the faithful old employee to use his flat on the top floor. It would be some relief for Sep to know that there was someone reliable living on the premises.

He telephoned to the mental hospital that morning to hear how Robert was, but learnt very little more than his mother's letter had told him. He had the chance, however, of talking to the doctor in charge of the case, and asked to be kept informed of his progress, explaining his own relationship and his desire to do anything to spare the patient's very old father.

As he replaced the receiver Edward noted, with a start of surprise, how anxious he was. Robert had never been very close to him. They were eleven years and a generation apart. By temperament they were opposed, and resentment, which had no place in Edward's life, ruled his young uncle's. But this was a blow at the whole family, and Edward's reaction had been swift and instinctive. It was all very well to decide to cut loose, he admitted somewhat wryly to himself, but the old tag about blood being thicker than water held good, as this shock had proved.

He resolved to go to Caxley at the weekend to see how things were for himself. Sep was pathetically delighted with the surprise visit, and Edward was glad to find that he was taking Robert's illness so bravely.

'I should have insisted on getting medical advice earlier,' he told Edward. 'Robert is certainly having proper treatment now, and perhaps a spell away from us will quicken his recovery.'

They talked of many things. Edward had never know him quite so forthcoming about the business. Perhaps he realized that Edward himself was now a keen and purposeful businessman. It certainly amazed the younger man to realize how profitable the old-established shop and the newer restaurant were, and what a grasp his grandfather had of every small detail in running them. Since Robert's departure, trade had improved. There were now no staff troubles with Kathy and John Bush in charge, and after a long day visiting his mother and grandmother, Bertie and Kathy, Edward drove back to London very much happier in mind.

His own business affairs he found engrossing. He

was now a partner in the firm, responsible chiefly for production and design. At his suggestion they had expanded their range of plastic kitchen equipment and were now experimenting with domestic refrigerators and larger deep-freeze receptacles for shops. This venture was proving amazingly successful and Edward found himself more and more absorbed and excited by the firm's development. Suddenly, after the apathy which had gripped him, he had found some purpose in life. He discovered a latent flair for design, an appreciation of line and form put to practical use, which gave him much inward satisfaction. The costing of a project had always interested him. He was, after all, the grandson of Bender North and Sep Howard, both men of business. He enjoyed planning a new design and then juggling with its economic possibilities. It was a fusion of two ways of thought and a new challenge every time it was undertaken.

He paid one or two visits to the continent to compare methods of production. He visited firms in Brussels and Paris who were engaged in much the same work as his own, and returned full of ideas. Jim and his father recognized that Edward was the most able of the three for this part of the business. His gaiety and charm, fast returning under the stimulus of new work, helped him to easy friendship. He had the ability to select ideas which could be adapted to their own business, and the power to explain them on his return to his partners. With Edward's drive, the firm was advancing rapidly.

In the early summer of 1947 Edward set off for a fortnight's visit to two firms in Milan. There were plumes of lilac blowing in the suburban gardens as the train rumbled towards the coast, and the girls were out and about in their pretty summer frocks. Edward approved of this 'new look' which brought back full skirts, neat waists, and gave women back the attractive curves which had been lost in the square military styles of wartime fashion. It was good to see colour and life returning to war-scarred England, to watch new houses being built, and see fresh paint brightening the old ones. There was hope again in the air, and the breezy rollicking tunes of the new musical Oklahoma exactly caught the spirit of the times – the looking-ahead of a great people to a future full of promise.

From Milan he made the long train journey to Venice, there to spend the last few days meeting an Italian industrial designer who lived there, and sight-seeing. From the moment that he emerged from the station into the pellucid brilliance of Venetian sunlight, he fell under the city's spell. The quality of the light, which revealed the details of brickwork and carving, exhilarated him. To take a gondola to one's hotel, instead of a prosaic bus or taxi, was wholly delightful. If only he could stay four months instead of four days!

His hotel was an agreeable one just off St Mark's Square. He looked from his window upon a gondola station. There were twenty or more black high-powered beauties jostling together upon the water. Their owners were busy mopping and polishing, shouting, laughing and gesticulating. Edward liked their energy, their raffish good looks and the torrents of words of which he only understood one in ten.

Picturesque though the scene was he was to find that its position had its drawbacks. The noise went on until one or two in the morning and began again about six. Luckily, Edward, healthily tired with walking about this enchanted place, did not lose much sleep.

On the last morning he awoke with a start. He was in the grip of some inexplicable fear. He found himself bathed in perspiration and his mind was perturbed with thoughts of Robert. He tossed back the bed clothes and lay watching the trembling reflections of the sun on water flickering across the ceiling. Against this undulating background he could see the face of Robert – a sad, haunted face, infinitely moving.

Outside, the gondoliers exchanged voluble jests in the bright Italian sunshine. The waters of Venice lapped against the walls and slapped the bottoms of the gondolas rhythmically. An Italian tenor poured forth a cascade of music from someone's wireless set.

But Edward was oblivious of his surroundings.

In that instant he was hundreds of miles away in the cool early dawn of an English market square. What was happening at home?

After breakfast he felt calmer. He packed his bags and paid his bill, glad to be occupied with small everyday matters and telling himself that he had simply suffered from a nightmare. But the nagging horror stayed with him throughout the long journey to England, and as soon as he arrived he rang his Uncle Bertie for news.

'Bad, I'm afraid,' said Bertie's voice, 'as you'll see when my letter arrives. Robert was found dead in the hospital grounds. They think he had a heart attack. We'll know more later.'

'When was this?' asked Edward.

Bertie told him. He must have died, thought Edward, as he had suspected, at the moment when he himself awoke so tormentedly in the hotel bedroom.

This uncanny experience had a lasting effect upon Edward's outlook. Hitherto impatient of anything occult, he, the least psychic of men, had discovered that not all occurrences could be rationally explained. It was to make him more sympathetic in the years to come and more humble in his approach to matters unseen.

Robert's tragic death had another effect on Edward's future. Unknown to him, Sep, when his first grief had passed, crossed the market square to enter the offices of Lovejoy and Lovejoy, his solicitors. There, the will which he had drafted so long ago was drastically revised, and when Sep returned to the bakery he was well content.

It was about this time that Edward heard that his ex-wife Angela had had a son by Billy Sylvester, her second husband. Edward was glad to hear the news. It should make Angela a happier person. Despite the misery which she had inflicted upon him, Edward felt no resentment. He soberly faced the fact that he could not exempt himself from blame. They had never had much in common, and it was largely physical attraction which had drawn them together. Now, with the baby to think of, she would have some interest in the future. Nevertheless, Edward felt a pang when he thought about the child. He might have had a son of his own if things had worked out.

But domesticity did not play much part in his present affairs, although he enjoyed running the little flat. He took most of his meals out, and he grew increasingly fond of London. His life-long love of the theatre could now be indulged, and by a lucky chance he was able to meet a number of theatrical people.

His Aunt Mary, younger sister of Bertie and his mother Winnie, and the acknowledged beauty of the family, had a small part in a well-written light comedy which had already run for eight months and looked as though it were settled in the West End for another two years. It was one of those inexplicable successes. No great names glittered in the cast, the play itself was not outstanding; but it was gay, the dialogue crisp, the settings and the costumes ravishing. It was just what theatre-goers seemed to want, and Aunt Mary hoped that they would continue to do so.

Edward took her out on several occasions after the show. He had always enjoyed her company, and found something exhilarating in the mixture of North common-sense, typified by his good-humoured Uncle Bertie, and the racy sophistication which her mode of life had added to it.

Two husbands, little mourned, lay in Aunt Mary's past. Many good friends of both sexes enlivened her present. She often brought one or more to Edward's supper parties, and he grew very fond of this animated company of friends, admiring the outward nonchalance which masked the resilience and dedication necessary to survive the ruthless competition of the stage world. They had something in common with businessmen, Edward decided. They needed to be long-sighted, ambitious and capable of grasping opportunity when it came. And, when times were hard, they must show the world a brave face to inspire confidence.

He liked to take out one or two of the pretty girls occasionally. It was good to laugh again, to be amused and to amuse in turn. He began to realize how little feminine company he had enjoyed. The war, early marriage, and the restrictions put upon him whilst awaiting his divorce, had combined with his temporary inner weariness to make him solitary. But although he enjoyed their company, there was not one among them with whom he would like to spend the rest of his days. The fact that they were equally heart-whole rendered them the more attractive.

More disturbing were the attentions of one of the girls who shared the flat above his own. As time passed, they had become better acquainted. Edward had used their telephone one evening when his own was out of order. He had stayed to coffee. Some evenings later they came to have a drink. From these small beginnings, not greatly encouraged by Edward, who enjoyed his domestic privacy, came more frequent visits by the girls.

Susan was engaged to a monosyllabic mountain of muscle who played Rugby football regularly on Wednesdays and Saturdays, and squash or badminton in between to keep himself fit for his place in the front row of the forwards. It was Elizabeth who was the more persistent of the two. She was small and dark, with an engaging cackling laugh, and Edward enjoyed her occasional company.

It was Elizabeth who called from the window, when he was gardening, offering him a drink. It was she who took in the parcels and delivered them to Edward when he returned from the office. And when he took to his bed with a short sharp bout of influenza it was Elizabeth who offered to telephone for the doctor and brought aspirins and drinks.

Edward, engrossed in his expanding business and intrigued with Aunt Mary's friends, had little idea of Elizabeth's growing affection. She was ardently stage-struck, and when she knew that Edward sometimes met people connected with the theatre, she grew pink with excitement. Edward found her touchingly young and unsophisticated. He invited her to come with him one evening to Aunt Mary's play, and to meet her afterwards.

It was a warm spring evening with London at its most seductive. A lingering sunset turned the sky to amethyst and turquoise. The costers' barrows were bright with daffodils, tulips and the first mimosa. In the brilliant shop windows, Easter brides trailed satin and lace. Hats as frothy as whipped egg-white, or as colourful as a handful of spring flowers, attracted the bemused window-gazers.

The play seemed to improve as its run lengthened, Edward thought. Aunt Mary queened it as becomingly as ever in all three acts. She was at her most sparkling afterwards at supper and brought a famous couple with her to dazzle Edward's young friend.

Later, while Edward was dancing with the actress and her husband was at the other side of the room talking with a friend, she watched Elizabeth's fond gaze follow Edward's handsome figure round the floor. He certainly was a personable young man, thought Aunt Mary, with family pride. He would have had a fine stage presence if he had cared to take up the profession.

'How well Edward fits into this sort of life,' said Elizabeth sighing. 'You can see that he loves London, and people, and a gay time.'

Aunt Mary, whose bright blue eyes missed nothing, either around her or in the human heart, seized her opportunity.

'I don't think you know Edward very well. He seems happy enough in town at the moment, but his roots are elsewhere. He doesn't know it yet himself, but Caxley will pull him back again before long. Of that I'm positive.'

'How can you say that?' protested Elizabeth. She looked affronted and hurt. 'What would Edward find in a poky little country town?'

'Everything worthwhile,' replied Aunt Mary composedly. 'He's his two Caxley grandfathers rolled into one, with a strong dash of my darling brother Bertie thrown in. That mixture is going to make a Caxley patriarch one day out of our dashing young Edward!'

'I don't believe it,' replied Elizabeth.

'Wait another ten years or so and you'll see,' promised Aunt Mary. But she felt quite certain that the pretty young thing beside her would not be prepared to wait at all. The role of country mouse would never do for her.

And that, thought Aunt Mary in her wisdom, was exactly as it should be.

## INTERLUDE IN IRELAND

While Edward enjoyed the spring in London, the good people of Caxley greeted the returning warmth just as heartily. At Rose Lodge, the clumps of daffodils and pheasant-eyed narcissi which Bender had planted, so long ago, were in splendid bloom. Bertie's garden, close by the Cax, was vivid with grape hyacinths and crocuses beneath the budding trees. Even Sep's small flagged yard, behind the bakehouse, sported a white-painted tub of early red tulips, put there by Kathy's hand.

Pale-pink sticks of rhubarb with yellow top-knots, the first pullets' eggs and bunches of primroses graced the market stalls. People were buying bright packets of flower seeds and discussing the rival merits of early potatoes. Felt hats were brushed and put away on top shelves, and straw ones came forth refurbished with new ribbon and flowers.

In the wide fields around Caxley the farmers were busy drilling and planting. Dim lights shone from lonely shepherds' huts as lambing continued. Along the hedges the honeysuckle and hawthorn put out their rosettes and fans of green, among the tattered tassels of the hazel catkins, and hidden beneath, the blue and white violets gave out the exquisite scent of spring from among their heart-shaped leaves.

Bertie, driving his mother to Beech Green one spring afternoon to visit her sister Ethel Miller, noticed the encouraging sights and sounds with a great sense of comfort. He always enjoyed being in this familiar countryside and remembered the long bicycle rides which he and the Howard brothers took when these same lanes were white with chalky dust and most of the traffic was horse-drawn.

It grieved him to see the new estates going up on the slopes flanking Caxley. People must be housed, but the gracelessness of the straight roads, the box-like structures packed too closely together, the narrow raw strips of gardens and the complete lack of privacy, saddened him. He would hate to have to live in a house like that, he thought, passing one garishly-painted one with a board outside saying: SHOW HOUSE, and he guessed that many future occupants would feel the same way, but be forced by circumstances to make the best of a bad job. It seemed to Bertie that for so little extra cost and care something lovely might have been built upon the fields he remembered, to give pleasure and pride to the dwellers there as well as to the town as a whole. As it was, this new development, in Bertie's opinion, was nothing but an eyesore and, as a block of houses embellished with moulded concrete weatherboarding came into view, he put his foot heavily on the accelerator to reach the sanctuary of leafy lanes beyond, unaltered since his boyhood.

It was good to arrive at the old farmhouse. Nothing seemed to have changed in the square panelled room which the Millers still called 'the parlour', and through the windows the copper beech, pink with young leaf, lifted its arms against the background of the mighty downs. Only such an observant eye as Bertie's would notice significant details of a fast-changing way of farming. Sacks of chemical fertilizer were stacked in a nearby barn. Strange new machinery had its place beside the old harvest binder which Bertie remembered his Uncle Jesse buying at a distant sale. Jesse's sons, it seemed, were abreast of modern methods.

The two old ladies gossiped of family affairs. There had been a letter that morning from Joan in Dublin.

'She's invited Edward to visit them later in the summer. That's the best of having a hotel, isn't it?'

'It could work both ways,' Bertie pointed out, amused at his mother's matter-of-fact approach. 'Suppose all your relations wanted to come for the summer. You wouldn't make much profit, would you?'

'Don't be tiresome, dear,' said his mother automatically, in the tone she had used ever since he could remember. Bertie smiled, and sampled his aunt's gingerbread in contented silence.

'Will he go?' asked Ethel. 'Who knows? He might meet a nice Irish girl.'

'Heaven forbid, Ethel! We've had quite enough mixed marriages in our family as it is!'

'They're not *all* Catholics over there,' said her sister with asperity. 'I know very well that quite a few of them are Christians.'

'You mean *Protestants*, surely, Aunt Ethel,' put in Bertie mildly. The old lady looked at him frostily and then transferred her gaze to her sister.

'That boy of yours, Hilda,' she observed severely, 'interrupts his elders and betters even more than he used to.'

'I'm so sorry,' said Bertie with due humility, and sat back with his gingerbread to play the role of listener only.

But, driving home again through the thickening twilight, Mrs North said:

'You mustn't mind what Ethel says, dear.'

'I don't, mamma,' replied Bertie calmly.

'She's getting old, you know, and a little peculiar in her ways.'

Bertie was about to say that Ethel was some years younger than she was herself, but had the sense to hold his tongue.

'Fancy suggesting that Edward might marry an

*Irish* girl!' There was an outraged air about this remark which amused Bertie. If Aunt Ethel had suggested that Edward was considering marriage with an aborigine, his mamma could not have sounded more affronted.

'Irish girls are quite famous for their charm and good looks,' said Bertie. 'But I don't think you need to worry about Edward. No doubt he can find a wife when he wants one.'

'If ever!' snapped old Mrs North shortly. Bridling, she turned to watch the hedges flying by, and spoke no more until Bertie deposited her again at Rose Lodge.

The invitation to Ireland pleased Edward mightily. He missed his sister Joan, for despite their promises to visit each other, various reasons had prevented them from meeting and it was now eighteen months since they had seen each other.

Business affairs would keep Edward ceaselessly engaged for the next two or three months, but he promised to cross to Ireland during the last week of August. It would be his first visit to a country which had always intrigued him. He hoped, if he could arrange matters satisfactorily at the factory, to go on from Dublin to see something of the west coast. He looked forward eagerly to the trip.

When the time came he set off in high spirits. He was to make the crossing from Holyhead to Dun Laoghaire, and as the train rattled across

Wales, Edward thought how little he knew of the countries which marched with his own. The war had fettered him, and for the last few years London had claimed him, apart from the occasional business trips abroad. Catching glimpses of Welsh mountains, and tumbling rivers so different from the placid Cax of home, he made up his mind that he would explore Wales and Scotland before he grew much older.

He slept soundly during the night crossing, and awoke to find the mailboat rocking gently in the great harbour of Dun Laoghaire, or Kingstown, as the old people at home still called it. Beyond the massive curves of the granite breakwaters, the little town basked in the morning sunshine. Gulls screamed above the glittering water. A maid twirled a mop from a window of the Royal Marine Hotel. A train, with a plume of smoke, chugged along the coast to Dublin. Edward's first glimpse of Ireland did not disappoint him.

He breakfasted aboard before meeting Joan and Michael who had driven the seven miles from Dublin to meet him.

'You both look younger – and fatter!' cried Edward with delight.

'It's Irish air and Irish food,' replied Joan, 'You see! You'll be twice the man at the end of your holiday.'

There was so much news to exchange on the drive to Dublin that Edward scarcely noticed his surroundings; but the soft, warm Irish air on his cheeks was strange and delicious.

Michael's father had died recently but his mother still made her home with them. Edward found her a gentler edition of his grandmother North, with some deafness which rendered her endearingly vague. Sarah, not yet two years old, with red curls and a snub nose, flirted outrageously with her uncle from the instant they met. She was in the care of a good-looking young nursemaid whose broad Irish speech Edward found entirely incomprehensible. She was equally incapable of understanding Edward, and for the duration of his stay they relied on smiles, and occasional interpretation from the family, for communication.

The hotel was small, but well placed in one of the quiet streets near Stephen's Green. Joan and Michael worked hard here and the business was thriving. Edward explored Dublin, mainly on his own, browsing at the bookstalls along the quays by the River Liffey, and admiring the humpbacked bridges which crossed its broad waters. Michael took time off from his duties to show him Trinity College, not far from the hotel, and Edward thought that the vast eighteenth-century library, its sombre beauty lit by slanting rays of sunlight, was one of the most impressive places he had ever seen.

On the third morning Joan received a letter

which she read at the breakfast table with evident satisfaction.

'She can come. Isn't that good?' she said to her husband.

'Maisie Hunter,' she told Edward. 'She's staying with an aunt in Belfast and said she would come down if she could manage it. She's arriving tomorrow by train.'

Although Edward liked Maisie, he felt a slight pang of regret. He was so much enjoying his present circumstances in this new place and among the friendly people who always seemed to have time to stop and talk with a curious stranger. At the moment he was content to forget Caxley and all its inmates. He chided himself for such selfishness and offered to meet Joan's friend at the station.

'Take the car,' said Michael. 'She's bound to have a mountain of luggage.'

But all Maisie carried were two neat matching cases when Edward first saw her, in the distance, stepping from the train. She was thinner than he remembered her, and her brown hair, which used to hang to her shoulders, was now short and softly curled. It suited her very well, thought Edward, hurrying to meet her. Her obvious surprise delighted him.

'I'd no idea you were here! What a nice surprise.'

Her smile was warm, lighting up her sun-tanned face and grey eyes. No one could call Maisie

Hunter a beauty: her features were not regular enough for such a description, but her skin and hair were perfect, and she had a vivacity of expression, combined with a low and lovely voice, which made her most attractive. Edward was now wholeheartedly glad to see her again.

'I've had a standing invitation to visit Joan,' she explained, as they drove towards Stephen's Green, 'and this seemed the right time to come. My aunt has her son and daughter arriving for a week's stay. But I didn't realize that I was interrupting a family reunion.'

Edward assured her truthfully that they were all delighted that she had come, and constituted himself as guide on this her first visit to Dublin.

'A case of the blind leading the blind,' he added, drawing up outside the hotel. 'But it's amazing how ready people are to drop what they are doing and take you wherever you want to go. Time stands still over here. That's Ireland's attraction to me.'

'You know what they say? "God made all the time in the world, and left most of it in Ireland." Now, where's my goddaughter?'

The next two or three days passed pleasantly. Edward and Maisie discovered the varied delights of Phoenix Park, revelling in the long walks across the windy central plain, watching the fine racehorses exercise and the little boys flying their kites in the warm summer breezes.

It was Michael who suggested that they took

his car and set off to explore the western part of Ireland.

'I've a good friend who has a little pub on the shores of Lough Corrib,' he told them. 'There's no such modern nonsenses as telephones there, but tell him I sent you. He'll find room for you, without doubt, and the views there will charm your hearts from your breasts.'

Michael, waxing lyrical in the Celtic fashion, always amused Edward. Ireland was the finest place in the world, Michael maintained, and it was a positive sin not to see as much of its glories as possible during Edward's short stay. Persuaded, the two set out in the borrowed car, promising to return in a few days.

Edward had envisaged hiring a car and making this journey on his own. He had secretly looked forward to this solitary trip, stopping when and where he liked, sight-seeing or not as the mood took him. But now that he had a companion he found that he was enjoying himself quite as much. They were easy together, sometimes talking animatedly, sharing memories of Caxley characters, or sometimes content to relax in silence and watch the rolling green fields of Ireland's central plain slide past.

The welcome at 'The Star' was as warm as Michael had promised. It was a small white-washed pub, set on a little knoll above the dark waters which reflected it. The sun was setting when they arrived, and long shadows streaked the calm surface of the lake. Edward thought that he had never seen such tranquility. His bedroom window looked across an expanse of grass, close-cropped by a dozen or so fine geese, to the lake. Here and there on the broad waters were islets, misty-blue against the darkening sky. Moored against the bank were three white skiffs, and Edward made up his mind to take one in the morning to explore those secret magical places fast slipping into the veils of twilight.

But now the welcome scent of fried bacon and eggs came drifting from below, and he hurried down, trying to dodge the low beams which threatened his head, to find Maisie and their waiting meal.

Their brief holiday passed blissfully. They explored Galway and made a trip to the Aran Islands in driving rain, and lost their hearts, just as Michael said they would, to the sad grey-green mountains and the silver beaches of Connemara. But it was the waters of Lough Corrib, lapping beneath their windows at night and supplying them with the most delicious trout and salmon of their lives, which had the strongest allure.

On their last day they took a picnic and set off in the boat to row across to one of the many islands. Maisie was taking a turn at the oars and Edward, eyes screwed up against the dazzling sunshine, watched her square brown hands tugging competently and thought how much he would miss her. He had been happier in her company than he would have thought possible. He tried to explain to himself why this should be. Of course they had known each other, off and on, for almost ten years, so that they had slipped into this unexpected companionship with perfect ease. And then there was no tiresome coquetry about the girl, no playing on her femininity. She had tackled the long walks, the stony mountain tracks, and the quagmires too, with enthusiasm and with no useless grieving over ruined shoes. He remembered an occasion when they descended a steep muddy lane beside a tiny farm, lured by the distant prospect far below of a shining beach. Out of the cottage had run a stout Irishwoman who threw up her hands in horror to see their struggles through the mud.

'Come away now,' she cried, 'and go down through our farm yard. You'll be destroyed that way!'

He laughed aloud at the memory.

'What now?' queried Maisie, resting on her oars. Bright drops slid down their length and plopped into the lake. He told her.

'Once when I was out with Philip,' she began animatedly, and then stopped. Edward watched her expression change swiftly from gaiety to sadness. This was the first time that she had mentioned her dead fiancé's name. They had not talked of their past at all during these few lovely days.

She looked away across the lake and spoke in

a low but steady voice, as though she had made up her mind to speak without restraint.

'Once when I was out with Philip,' she repeated, and continued with the anecdote. But Edward did not hear it. He was too engrossed with his own thoughts. From his own experience, he guessed that this moment was one of great advance for Maisie's progress towards full recovery from her grief. If Ireland had been able to thaw the ice which held her heart, then that alone would make this holiday unforgettable.

He became conscious that she was silent, and smiling at him.

'You haven't heard a word, have you?' she asked. 'Don't fib. I don't mind. D'you know that something wonderful has just happened to me?'

'Yes,' said Edward gently. 'I can guess.'

'I've never spoken about him. I couldn't. But somehow, here, with nothing but lake and sky, it seems easy. My family mind so much for me, I don't dare to talk of it. I can't face the emotion it brings forth.'

'I've had my share of that,' replied Edward. 'Someone – I think it was Uncle Bertie – told me once that it's the hardest thing in the world to receive pity. The damnable thing is that it takes so many forms – and all of them hell for the victim.'

He found himself telling the girl about his own family's attitude to his broken marriage, and the comfort he had found in his solitary life.

'We've been lucky in having that,' agreed Maisie. 'My Caxley flat has been a haven. I should have gone mad if I had been living at home. There's a lot to be said for a single existence. Wasn't it Katherine Mansfield who said that living alone had its compensations? And that if you found a hair in your honey it was a comfort to know it was your own?'

An oar slipped from its rowlock and the boat rocked.

'Here, let me row for a bit,' said Edward, restored to the present. They crept gingerly past each other exchanging places, and Edward pulled steadily towards the nearest island.

They picnicked on salmon and cucumber sandwiches and hard-boiled eggs, afterwards lying replete in the sun. A moorhen piped from the reeds nearby. The sun was warm upon their closed eyes. A little breeze shivered upon the surface of the lake and ruffled their hair.

'Damn going back,' said Edward lazily. 'I could stay here for ever.'

'Me too,' said Maisie ungrammatically. 'I feel quite different. You've been a great help, letting me talk about Philip. It was a thousand pities we never married, in more ways than one. Somehow one tends to build up a sort of deity from the person one's lost, and I think that is wrong. If we'd had a few years of married ups and downs perhaps I should have been able to bear it more bravely.'

'In some ways,' said Edward, 'you miss them more.' He remembered, with sharp poignancy, the perfume which Angela had used and how terribly it had affected him after their parting.

He propped himself on one elbow and looked down upon his companion. She looked very young and vulnerable, a long grass clamped between her teeth, her eyes shut against the sunlight. She'd had a tough road to travel, just as he had. Fortunately, he was further along that stony track, and knew that, in the end, it grew easier. He tried to tell her this.

'It gets better, you know, as you go on. All that guff about Time, the Great Healer, which irritates one so when one's still raw – well, it's perfectly true. I've just got out of the let-me-lick-my-wound-in-solitude state, which you're still in, and all the things which wise old people like Sep told me are coming true. Hope comes back, and purpose, and a desire to do something worthwhile – and, best of all, the perfectly proper feeling that it is *right* to be happy, and not to feel guilty when cheerfulness breaks in.'

Maisie opened her grey eyes, threw aside the grass and smiled at him.

'Dear Edward,' she said, 'you are an enormous comfort.'

They returned reluctantly to Dublin. Edward was to go back the next day to England. Maisie was going to her aunt's for a little longer.

'When do you go back to Caxley?' asked

Edward, through the car window as Michael prepared to drive him to the station.

'Term starts on September the twelfth,' said Maisie. 'A Thursday. I'll probably go back on Tuesday or Wednesday.'

'I shall be down on Friday evening for the weekend,' said Edward with decision. 'Keep it free. Promise?'

'Promise,' nodded Maisie, as the car drove away.

## EDWARD AND MAISIE

During the golden autumn months that followed Edward's visit to Ireland, work at the factory quickened its pace. Edward was as enthusiastic and conscientious as ever, but it did not escape the eyes of his partners that all his weekends were now spent at Caxley.

Elizabeth, in the flat above, watched Edward's car roar away early on Saturday mornings, or sometimes on Friday evenings, when pressure of work allowed. Aunt Mary, it seemed, was right when she predicted that Caxley would pull her attractive nephew homeward. What was she like, Elizabeth wondered, this Caxley girl who had succeeded where she had failed?

Not that she cared very much, she told herself defiantly. There were just as good fish in the sea, and the thought of spending her life in a tin-pot little dump like Caxley appalled her.

If Edward wanted to bury himself alive in a place like that, then she was glad that nothing had come of their affair. It was only, she admitted wistfully, that he was so extraordinarily handsome, and made such a wonderful escort. Meanwhile, it was no good grieving over her losses. Sensibly, she turned her attention to the other young men in her life. They might not have quite the same high standard of good looks and general eligibility as dear, lost Edward, but they were certainly more attainable.

In Caxley, of course, the tongues wagged briskly. The Howards had provided gossip of one sort or another for generations. There was that deliciously spicy affair of Sep's wife Edna, the Caxley folk reminded each other, when Dan Crockford painted her portrait and the shameless hussy had sat for it *unchaperoned*. True, she was fully dressed, they added, with some disappointment in their tones, but Sep had been very upset about it at the time. It had happened years ago, in the reign of King Edward the Seventh in fact, but was still fresh in the memories of many old stalwarts of the market square.

Sep's rise in fortune was remembered too, and the buying of Bender North's old property, but there were few who grudged Sep his success. He bore himself modestly and his high principles were respected. Besides, he had faced enough trouble in his life with the death of his first-born in the war, and the going's-on of his second son Leslie. It must be hard to banish one's child, as Sep had done. Did he ever regret it, they asked each other? And then this last tragedy of poor Robert's! What a burden Sep had carried to be sure!

But this latest tit-bit was a pleasant one. It was a pity, of course, that Maisie Hunter was not a true-bred Caxley girl, but only a war-time arrival. On the other hand, as one pointed out to her neighbour over the garden hedge, a bit of fresh blood worked wonders in these old inter-married families of Caxley. And say what you like, if Maisie Hunter had chosen to stay all these years in Caxley, it proved that she had good sense and that she was worthy to marry into their own circle. It was to be hoped, though, that the children would take after Edward for looks. Maisie Hunter was *healthy* enough, no doubt, but certainly no oil painting – too skinny by half.

Thus flowed the gossip, but one important point was overlooked by the interested bystanders. It was taken for granted that Maisie Hunter would accept such a fine suitor with alacrity. The truth was that Edward's ardent and straightforward wooing was meeting with severe set-backs. Maisie was beset with doubts and fears which were as surprising to Edward as they were painful to the girl herself.

Was he truly in love with her, or simply ready

for domesticity? Was he prompted by pity for her circumstances? The questions beat round and round in her brain, and she could find no answer.

She wondered about her own response. In the solitude of the little flat which had become so dear to her, she weighed the pros and cons of the step before her, in a tumult of confusion. She was now twenty-nine, and Edward was two years older. There was a lot to give up if she married. She was at the peak of a career she enjoyed. The idea of financial dependence was a little daunting, and she would hate to leave Caxley. She was not at all sure that she wanted to embark on the troubled seas of motherhood as soon as she married, and yet it would be best for any children they might have to start a family before she and Edward were much older.

And then, to be a *second* wife was so much more difficult than to be a *first*. Marriage, for Edward, had been such an unhappy episode. Could she make him as happy as he deserved to be? Would he secretly compare her with his first wife? Would he find her equally disappointing and demanding? Wouldn't it be safer if they didn't marry after all, she wondered, in despair?

It had all been so much simpler when she had become engaged to Philip. They had both been very young. Love, marriage, and children had seemed so simple and straightforward then. Now everything was beset with doubts and complications. Philip's death had shaken her world so deeply, that any decision was difficult to make. Edward's patience with her vacillations made her feel doubly guilty. It was not fair to subject him to such suspense, but she could not commit herself while she was so tormented.

Thus the autumn passed for Maisie in a strange blur of intense happiness and horrid indecision. Edward came to see her each weekend, and often she travelled to London to meet him after school. In his company she was at peace, but as soon as she returned to Caxley the nagging questions began again. The Howards and Norths were dismayed at the delay in Edward's plans. It was quite apparent that he was in love. What on earth could Maisie be thinking of to shilly-shally in this way? Wasn't their Edward good enough for her?

November fogs shrouded the market square. The Cax flowed sluggishly, reflecting sullen skies as grey as pewter. People hurried home to their firesides, looked out hot-water bottles, took to mufflers, complained of rheumatic twinges, and faced the long winter months with resignation. The gloom was pierced on November 14 that year by the news of the birth of a son to the Princess Elizabeth. The church bells rang in the market square, and from village towers and steeples in the countryside around. Their joyous clamour was in Maisie's ears as she pushed a letter to Joan into the pillar box at the corner of the market place.

It had taken her a long time to write, but even

longer to decide if it should be written at all. But it was done, and now relief flooded her. All the things which she had been unable to tell Edward, she had written to his sister, and she begged for advice as unbiased as possible in the circumstances. Maisie respected Joan's good sense. In these last few agitated weeks, she had longed to talk with her, to discuss her doubts with someone of her own sex, age and background.

She awaited the reply from Ireland with as much patience as she could muster. No doubt Joan would take as much time and trouble with her answer as she herself had taken in setting out her problems. As the days passed, she began to wonder if it had been kind to press Joan on the matter. After all, she was an exceptionally busy person, and young Sarah took much of her attention.

At last the letter came. Maisie sped to the door, her breakfast coffee untasted. It lay, a square white envelope with the Irish stamp, alone on the door mat. Trembling, Maisie bent to pick it up. It was thin and light. Obviously, whatever message Joan sent was going to prove terse and to the point. She tore it open. Joan's neat handwriting covered only one side of the paper.

You darling ass,

All your ifs and buts are on Edward's account, I notice. Let him shoulder his own worries, if he has any, which I doubt – and please say 'Yes.' Go ahead and just be happy, both of you.

All our love,<br>Joan

P.S. Dr Kelly has just confirmed our hopes. Prepare for a christening next April.

Suddenly, the bleak November morning seemed flooded with warmth and light. This was exactly the right sort of message to receive – straightforward, loving and wise. How terrible, Maisie realized, it would have been to receive a long screed putting points for and against the marriage – merely a prolongation of the dreary debate which had bedevilled her life lately. Joan had summed up the situation at once, had recognized the nervous tension which grew more intense as time passed and had made Maisie's decision impossible. In a few lines she had pointed out something simple and fundamental to which worry had blinded her friend. Edward knew what he was undertaking. Maisie recalled his saying one evening, with a wry smile: 'You might give me credit for some sense. I've thought about it too, you know.'

She folded the letter, put it in her handbag like a talisman, and set off, smiling, for school.

'No long engagement for us,' said Edward firmly next weekend. 'You might change your mind again, and that I couldn't face.'

They had spent the winter afternoon visiting the family to tell them of their engagement and their future plans.

At Rose Lodge it was Grandma North who received the news with the greatest display of excitement.

'At last, a wedding in St Peter's!' she exclaimed, clapping her thin papery old hands together. Edward shook his head.

'Afraid not. For one thing we neither of us want it. And I don't think our vicar would relish a divorced man at his altar.'

'Not a church wedding?' faltered the old lady. 'Oh, what a disappointment! Really, it does seem hard!'

She rallied a little, and her mouth took on the obstinate curve which Edward knew so well.

'I'll have a word with the vicar myself, dear boy. Bender and I worked for the church all our lives, and the least he can do is to put on a nice little wedding service for our grandson.' She spoke as if the vicar would be arranging a lantern lecture in the church hall – something innocuous and sociable – with coffee and Marie biscuits to follow.

Edward broke into laughter. His grandmother began to pout, and he crossed the room in three strides and kissed her heartily. Unwillingly, she began to smile, and Winnie, watching them both, thought how easily Edward managed the wilful old lady whose autocratic ways grew more pronounced and embarrassing as the years passed.

'No, no church this time, but a wonderful wedding party at Sep's. He's already planning the cake decorations, and we shall expect your prettiest bonnet on the day.'

Mrs North appeared mollified, and turned her attention to more practical matters concerning linen, silver and china. It was clear that she was going to be busily engaged in the wedding preparations from now on.

And this time, thought Winnie, her eyes upon Edward and Maisie, there is happiness ahead. For a fleeting moment she remembered her first encounter with Angela, and the dreadful premonition of disaster to come. Now, just as deeply, she felt that this time all would be well for them both.

Sep too, had shared the same feeling when he had held their hands that afternoon and congratulated them.

'Dear boy, dear boy!' he repeated, much moved. His welcome to Maisie was equally warm. He had known and liked her for many years now. She would make Edward a good wife.

He accompanied them down the stairs from his parlour above the shop and said good-bye to them in front of the bow windows which displayed the delicious products of his bakehouse at the back. When they were out of sight, he glanced across at the fine windows above his restaurant across the square. Would Edward ever return there, he wondered? Would his children gaze down one day upon the varied delights of market day, as Edward had done, and his friend Bender's children had done, so long ago, when horses had clip-clopped across the cobbles and Edward the Seventh was on the throne?

He turned to look with affection at that monarch's mother, small and dignified, surveying the passing traffic from her plinth.

'No one like her,' exclaimed Sep involuntarily. 'No one to touch her, before or since.'

Two schoolgirls, chewing toffee, giggled together and nudged each other. What a silly old man, talking to himself! They passed on, unseen by Sep.

He entered the shop, glad to be greeted by its fragrant warmth after the raw cold outside. For four reigns now he had served in this his own small kingdom. Sometimes, lately, he had wondered if he could rule for much longer, but now, with Edward's good news ringing in his ears, he felt new strength to face the future.

'I'll take some crumpets for tea,' he said to the assistant behind the scrubbed counter.

He mounted the stairs slowly, bearing his paper bag to Miss Taggerty. This, after all, he told himself, was the right way for a baker to celebrate.

The wedding was to be in January, and meanwhile Edward searched for a house or a larger flat than the one in which he now lived. Maisie accompanied him as often as her school work would allow.

It was a dispiriting task. New houses had gone up in abundance near Edward's factory, but neither he nor Maisie could face their stark ugliness, the slabs of raw earth waiting to be transformed into tiny gardens and the complete lack of privacy. Older houses, in matured gardens, never seemed to be for sale.

Back in Edward's little flat after an exhausting foray, Maisie kicked off her shoes and gazed round the room.

'What's wrong with this?' she asked.

'Why, nothing,' said Edward, 'except that it's hardly big enough for one, let alone two.'

'We haven't seen anything as comfortable as this,' replied Maisie. 'I'll be happy here, if you will. Let's start here anyway. If it becomes impossible we'll think again – but I simply can't look at any more places just now. I can't think why we didn't settle for this in the first place.'

Edward agreed, with relief. It might not be ideal, but the flat was quiet with an outlook upon grass and trees, and it would be simple for Maisie to run. He would like to have found something more splendid for his new wife, but their recent expeditions had proved daunting, to say the least. Maybe, in time, they could move much further away, to the pleasant greenness of Buckinghamshire, perhaps, where property was attractive and the daily journey to work would not be too arduous. Meanwhile, Edward's tiny flat, refurbished a little by Maisie, would be their first home.

There was snow on the ground on their wedding day, but the sun shone from a pale-blue cloudless sky. Steps and window sills were edged with white, and the pigeon's coral feet made hieroglyphics on the snowy pavements. Edward and Maisie emerged from the registrar's office into the market place, dazzled with the sunshine, the snow and their own happiness.

'I suppose,' said Mrs North to Bertie, as they followed the pair, 'that it's *legal*. I mean they *really are* married?'

'Perfectly legal, mamma,' Bertie assured her.

'It seems so *quick*,' protested the old lady. 'I do so hope you're right, Bertie. It would be terrible for them to find they were living in sin.'

The registrar, coming upon the scene and overhearing this remark, gave a frosty bow and marched stiffly away.

'Now you've offended him,' said Bertie, smiling.

'Hm!' snorted the old lady, unrepentant. 'Marrying people without even a surplice! Small wonder he hurries away!'

It was a gay party that gathered in Sep's restaurant. The wedding cake stood on a table by the windows which overlooked the snowy garden. The dark waters of the Cax gleamed against the white banks, and a robin perching upon a twig peered curiously at the array of food inside the window.

Edward gazed contentedly about him. Sep and his grandmother were nodding sagely across the table. Her wedding hat was composed of velvet pansies in shades of blue and violet. She had certainly succeeded in finding a beauty, thought Edward affectionately.

His mother and Bertie were in animated conversation. Aunt Kathy, gorgeous in rose-pink, glowed at the corner of the table, her children nearby. If only Joan could have been here it would have been perfect, but he and Maisie were to see her before long as they returned from their honeymoon.

He turned to look at his new wife. She wore a soft yellow suit and looked unusually demure. He laughed and took her hand. Another Howard had joined the family in the market square.

Far away, the quiet waters of Lough Corrib reflected the bare winter trees growing at the lake side.

There was no snow here. A gentle wind rustled the dry reeds, and the three white skiffs lay upside down on the bank, covered by a tarpaulin for the winter. The grey and white geese converged upon the back door of the inn, necks outstretched, demanding food.

A plume of blue smoke curled lazily towards the winter sky. Timeless and tranquil, 'The Star' gazed at its reflection in the water, and awaited its guests.

## HARVEST LOAVES

One bright Sunday morning in April, Sep awoke with curious constriction in his chest. He lay still, massaging it gently with a small bony hand. He was not greatly perturbed. A man in his eighties expects a few aches and pains, and Sep had always made light of his ailments.

It was fortunate, he thought, that it was Sunday. On weekdays he continued to rise betimes, despite his family's protests, but on Sunday he allowed himself some latitude and Miss Taggerty prepared breakfast for eight o'clock.

Always, when he awoke, his first thoughts were of Edna. He lay now, remembering just such a shining morning, when he and Edna had taken the two boys for a picnic in the woods at Beech Green. Robert and Kathy were not born then, and Jim and Leslie had frisked before them like young lambs, along the lane dappled with sunshine and shadow. They had picked bunches of primroses, and eaten their sandwiches in a little clearing. Sep could see the young birch trees now, fuzzy with green-gold leaf. A pair of blackbirds had flown back and forth to their nestlings, and a young rabbit had lolloped across the clearing, its fur silvered and its translucent ears pink, in the bright sunshine.

Perhaps he remembered it so clearly, thought Sep, because they so rarely had a day out together. The shop had always come first. Edna must have found it a great tie sometimes, but he could not recall her complaining. She had been a wonderful wife. He missed her more and more. It was hard to grow old alone.

He sat up, suddenly impatient with his own self-pity, and a spasm of pain shot through him. It was so sharp and unexpected that he gasped in dismay. When it had abated a little, he lay back gingerly against the pillow. The bells of St Peter's were ringing for early service. It would soon be seven-thirty.

'Indigestion,' Sep told himself aloud. He tried to remember if he had eaten anything unusual on the previous day, but failed. His appetite was small, and he had never been in the habit of eating a heavy meal in the evening. Perhaps he had put too much sugar in his Horlicks. As he grew older he found himself becoming increasingly fond of sweet things. He must not be so self-indulgent.

He sat up carefully. The pain was dwindling, and he crossed slowly to the window. A few church-goers were mounting the steps of St Peter's. A milkman's float clanged and jangled on the opposite side of the square. It was a typical Sunday morning in Caxley – a scene which he had looked upon hundreds of times and always taken for granted.

But today, suddenly, it had a poignant significance for Sep. Would he see many more Sundays? Death must come soon, and he was unafraid – but Caxley was very dear, and hard to leave behind.

He shaved and dressed carefully in his sober Sunday suit in readiness for chapel, and in his mind there beat a line of poetry which he had heard only that week.

> Look they last on all things lovely,
> Every hour –

It was good sense, Sep decided, descending the stairs slowly, as well as good poetry.

In the weeks that followed, the pain recurred. Sep found that his head swam sometimes when he bent down, or if he lifted a heavy pan in the bakehouse. He told no one of the disability, dismissing it as a passing ailment, unworthy of serious attention. He brushed aside Miss Taggerty's anxious inquiries. There was little affecting her master which her keen old eyes missed, but natural timidity kept her from expressing her fears to the rest of the family. Sep would brook no tale-telling, she knew well.

But the secret could not be kept for long. One

warm May evening Sep set off along the tow path to see Kathy and Bertie. Half a dozen naked boys splashed and shouted by the further bank. Clouds of midges drifted above the river, and swallows swooped back and forth, like dark blue arrows. From the oak tree near Bertie's garden gate, minute green caterpillars jerked on their gossamer threads. It was sultry, with a mass of dark clouds building up menacingly on the horizon. Soon there would be thunder, and the boys would scramble for home, leaving the placid surface of the river to be pitted with thousands of drops.

Bertie was in his vegetable garden, spraying the blackfly from his broad beans. Sep heard the rhythmic squish-squish of the syringe. Bertie was hidden from sight by a hawthorn hedge which divided the lawn from the kitchen garden. A blackbird flew out, squawking frenziedly, as Sep brushed the hedge. There were probably a dozen or more nests secreted in its length, Sep surmised, looking at it with interest. He turned to watch his son-in-law, still unaware of his presence, intent on washing away the sticky black pest.

Bertie wore well, he thought affectionately. His figure had thickened slightly, and his hair, still plentiful, had turned to silver. But his complexion was fresh and his blue eyes as bright as ever. He was becoming more like Bender as he grew older, but would never have the girth, or the bluster, of his father. Bender's ebullience had made Sep nervous at times. There was nothing to fear in his son.

At last he straightened up, and started when he saw Sep's slight figure at the end of the row.

'Good heavens! I didn't hear you arrive! How are you? Let me put this thing away and we'll go indoors.'

'No, no, my boy. Finish the job. There's rain on the way and there's no hurry on my account.'

Obediently, Bertie refilled his syringe and set off along the last row, Sep following. A flourishing plant of groundsel caught the old man's eye and he bent to pull it up. Immediately, the pain in his chest had him in its grip with such intensity that his head thumped. The rosette of groundsel, the damp earth and the pale green stalks of the bean plants whirled round and round together, growing darker and darker, as the blood pounded in his head.

Bertie ran to pick up the old man who was in a dead faint and gasping alarmingly. His cheek and the grey hair at one temple were muddied by the wet soil. With difficulty Bertie managed to lift him in his arms and limped towards the house, calling for Kathy. Sep was as light as a bird, Bertie noticed, despite his agitation – lighter by far than his own young son, Andrew.

They put him on the couch and Kathy ran for smelling salts, while Bertie chafed the frail hands and watched him anxiously.

'We must call the doctor,' he said. As he spoke, Sep opened his eyes and shook his head slowly and wearily.

'No. No doctor,' he whispered.

'Some brandy?' urged Bertie.

'No, thank you,' said Sep, with a touch of his old austerity. Bertie realized that he had blundered.

'Some tea then?'

Sep nodded and closed his eyes again. Kathy ran to the kitchen and Bertie followed her.

'Whatever he says, I'm ringing for the doctor. This is something serious, I feel sure.'

Within ten minutes the doctor had arrived. There was no demur from Sep who, with the tea untasted, lay frail and shrunken against Kathy's bright cushions, with a blanket tucked around him. The examination over, the doctor spoke with false heartiness.

'You'll see us all out, Mr Howard. Just a tired heart, but if you take care of yourself, you'll be as sound as a bell for years yet. I'll write you a prescription.'

Bertie accompanied him into the lane, well out of ear-shot.

'Tell me the truth, doctor. How is he?'

'As I said. If he takes his pills regularly and avoids excessive exercise, he can tick over for a few more years. Your job is to persuade him to take things easily.'

'That's one of the hardest things in the world

to ask me to do, but I'll try. Should he spend the night here?'

'It would be best. Tell him to stay there until I call again in the morning.'

Sep submitted to the doctor's orders with unusual docility, and as soon as he was settled in Kathy's spare room Bertie hurried to the market square to tell the news to Miss Taggerty.

It grieved Sep, in the months that followed, to lead such a comparatively inactive life. True, he rose at the usual time and supervised the shop, the restaurant, and the bakehouse, as he had always done, but he walked from place to place more slowly now, and tried not to mount his steep stairs more than was necessary. The doctor had advised him to rest after his midday dinner, and now that the weather was warm, he took to sitting in the old arbour by the river at the rear of the restaurant. This had been his old friend Bender's favourite spot, and Sep had made sure that it was kept as spruce as Bender would have wished.

Jasmine starred and scented its rustic entrance, and an Albertine rose added its splendour. Kathy made the rough seat comfortable with cushions, and provided a footstool and rug. It was a perfect sun trap, and as she went about her affairs in the restaurant, she could watch Sep dozing in sheltered warmth, or gazing at his life-long companion, the river Cax.

The family called to see Sep more often than

usual. Hilda North took to paying Sep an occasional afternoon visit. Winnie drove her down the hill from Rose Lodge and left her to keep the old man company while she shopped in the town.

The two old people, who shared so many common memories, were closer now than ever they had been, and as they took tea together in the arbour they enjoyed reminiscing about their early days in the market square when their children had played together in this same garden, and floated their toy boats on the river before them.

Edward and Maisie spent as many weekends in Caxley as they could, but both were busy, for Maisie had taken a part-time teaching post. Miss Hedges, the middle-aged headmistress who lived in a neighbouring flat, had soon discovered that Maisie was a trained teacher, and had no difficulty in persuading her to accompany her three mornings a week to school. Here Maisie helped children who were backward in reading and thoroughly enjoyed the work.

'But we don't call them "backward" these days, my dear,' said Miss Hedges with a twinkle. ' "Less able" is the most forthright term we are allowed to use in these namby-pamby times!'

Maisie was glad to be doing something worthwhile again. She and Edward were blissfully happy, but he was off to work before half-past eight, the tiny flat was set to rights soon after, and Maisie was beginning to find time hanging heavily on her hands when Miss Hedges had appeared. It was a happy arrangement for them all.

Maisie found her new life absorbing. She looked back now upon her doubts and fears with amusement and incredulity. How right Joan had been, and how lucky she was to have found Edward! They had much in common. As a Londoner, Maisie shared Edward's love of the theatre and they spent many evenings there. Aunt Mary, going from strength to strength as she became better known as a character actress, saw them frequently, and was loud in her approval of Edward's choice.

'And when are you going to Caxley?' she inquired one September evening, after the play. She was in her dressing-room removing make-up with rapid expert strokes.

'The weekend after next,' replied Edward.

'I meant for good,' said his aunt. She noted Edward's surprise.

'Hadn't really thought about it,' said Edward frankly. 'This job is growing daily, and the journey from Caxley would take too long. We're still hoping for a house in the country somewhere, but it will have to be nearer than Caxley.'

Aunt Mary did not pursue the subject. How it would come about she did not know, but in her bones she felt quite sure that Edward and his Maisie were destined for Caxley one day.

She rose from her seat before the dressing table and kissed them unexpectedly.

'Give the old place my love,' she said. 'And all the people who remember me there. Particularly Sep – yes, particularly Sep!'

The last Friday in September was as warm and golden as the harvest fields through which Edward and Maisie drove to Caxley. It had been a good crop this year and the weather had been favourable. Most of the fields were already cut, and the bright stubble bristled cleanly in the sunshine.

Winnie was staking Michaelmas daisies in the garden of Rose Lodge when they arrived. Edward thought how well she looked, and his grandmother too, as they sipped their sherry and exchanged news.

'And Sep?' asked Edward.

'Fairly well,' said his grandmother. 'I had tea with him yesterday afternoon and he's looking forward to seeing you.'

'I'll go and have a word with him now,' said Edward. 'Coming?' he asked Maisie.

'Tell him I'll look in tomorrow morning,' she answered. 'I'll unpack and help here.'

'Don't be long,' called Winnie as he made for the car.

'There's a chicken in the oven, and it will be ready by eight o'clock.'

'That's a date,' shouted Edward cheerfully, driving off.

The long shadow of St Peter's spire stretched across the market place, but the sun still gleamed warmly upon Sep's shop and the windows of his house above it. Edward parked the car and looked around him with satisfaction. Choir practice was in session and he could hear the singers running through the old familiar harvest hymns. Queen Victoria wore a pigeon on her crown and looked disapproving. At the window of his own flat he could see old John Bush, peering at a newspaper held up to the light. This was the time of day when Sep's house had the best of it, Edward thought, and remembered how, as a boy, he had explained to his grandfather why he preferred Bender's old home to Sep's.

'It gets the sun most of the day,' he had told the old man. 'You only get it in the evening.'

But how it glorified everything, to be sure! The western rays burnished Sep's side of the square, gilding steps and door-frames and turning the glass to sheets of fire. Edward ran up the stairs, at the side of the closed shop, and called to his grandfather. Miss Taggerty greeted him warmly.

'He's pottering about downstairs, Mr Edward, having a final look at the Harvest Festival loaves, no doubt. The chapel folk are fetching them tomorrow morning for the decorations. Lovely they are! He did them himself. You'll find him there, you'll see.'

Edward made his way to the bakehouse. There was no one about at this time of day and the yard was very quiet. He entered the bakehouse and was greeted by the clean fragrance of newly-baked bread which had been familiar to him all his life. Ranged against the white wall stood two splendid loaves in the shape of sheaves of corn, with smaller ones neatly lined up beside them. There were long plaited loaves, fat round ones, Coburg, cottage, split-top – a beautiful array of every pattern known to a master baker.

And sitting before them, at the great table white and ribbed with a lifetime's scrubbing, was their creator. He was leaning back in his wooden arm chair, his hands upon the table top and his gaze upon his handiwork. He looked well content.

But when Edward came to him he saw that the eyes were sightless and the small hands cold in death. There, in the centre of his world, his lovely work about him and his duty done, Sep rested at last.

Dazed and devastated, an arm about his grandfather's frail shoulders, Edward became conscious of the eerie silence of the room. Across the square the sound of singing drifted as the boys in St Peter's choir practised their final hymn.

'*All is safely gathered in,*' they shrilled triumphantly, as the long shadows reached towards Sep's home.

# PROBLEMS FOR EDWARD

In the bewildered hours that followed Sep's death, the family began to realize just how deeply they would miss his presence. He had played a vital part in the life of each one. He had been the lynch-pin holding the Norths and Howards together, and his going moved them all profoundly.

After the first shock was over, Edward and Bertie spent the weekend making necessary arrangements for the funeral, writing to friends and relatives, drafting a notice for *The Caxley Chronicle* and coping with the many messages of sympathy from the townsfolk who had known Sep all his life.

As they sat at their task, one at each end of Bertie's dining-room table, Bertie looked across at Edward. The younger man was engrossed in his writing, head bent and eyes lowered. His expression was unusually solemn, and in that moment Bertie realized how very like Sep's was his cast of countenance. There was something in the slant of the cheekbone and the set of the ear which recalled the dead man clearly. Age would strengthen the likeness as Edward's hair lost its colour and his face grew thinner.

There was also, thought Bertie, the same concentration on the job in hand. Edward had assumed this sudden responsibility so naturally that, for the first time, he felt dependent upon the younger man. He had slipped into his position of authority unconsciously, and it was clear to Bertie that Edward henceforth would be the head of the family. It was a thought which flooded Bertie with rejoicing and relief. It was all that Sep had hoped for in his wisdom.

The chapel in the High Street was full on the occasion of Sep's funeral. Edward had not realized how many activities Sep had taken part in in the town. He was a councillor for many years. He had been a member of the hospital board, the Red Cross committee, the Boys' Brigade, and a trustee of several local charities. All these duties he had performed conscientiously and unobtrusively. It was plain, from the large congregation, that Sep's influence was widely felt and that he would be sorely missed in Caxley's public life.

The coffin bore the golden flowers of autumn. The chapel was still decorated with the corn and trailing berries of Harvest Festival. Edward, standing between Maisie and his mother, with Kathy beautiful in black nearby, was deeply moved, and when, later, Sep was lowered into the grave beside his adored wife, the dark cypress trees and bright flowers of Caxley's burial ground were blurred by unaccustomed tears. Sep had been a father as well as a grandfather to him. It was doubly hard to say farewell.

But, driving back to Bertie and Kathy's after the ceremony, he became conscious of a feeling of inner calm. This was death as it should be – rest after work well done, port after storm. Death, as Edward had met it first during the war, was violent and unnatural, the brutal and premature end of men still young. Sep had stayed his course, and the memory of that serene dead face gave his grandson comfort now, and hope for the future.

He and Maisie said little on the journey back to town, but later that evening Maisie spoke tentatively.

'Did you wish – did you feel – that your father should have been there, Edward?'

'Yes, I did,' replied Edward seriously. 'As a matter of fact, I wrote to him and told him.'

'Where is he then? I'd no idea you knew where he was!'

'I haven't. Mother would never speak of him – nor, of course, would Sep. But I found an address among his papers when Uncle Bertie and I were putting things straight. Somewhere in Devon. Heaven alone knows if he's still there, but it might be sent on to him, if he's moved. I felt he should know.'

It was the first time that his father had been mentioned, though Maisie knew well the story of Leslie Howard's flight with an earlier love when Edward was only four and Joan still a baby in arms.

'Do you remember him?'

'Hardly at all. I can remember that he used to swing me up high over his head, which I liked. The general impression is a happy one, strangely enough. He was full of high spirits – probably slightly drunk – but willing to have the sort of rough-and-tumble that little boys enjoy.'

'And you've never wanted to see him again?'

'Sometimes, yes. Particularly when I was about sixteen or so. Luckily, Uncle Bertie was at hand always, so he got landed with my problems then. And I knew mother would have hated to see him again, or to know that I'd been in touch. As for Grandma North, I think she would have strangled my father with her bare hands if she'd clapped eyes on him again! He certainly behaved very badly to his family. Sep minded more than anyone. That's why he never spoke of him. He was such a kind man that I always thought it was extraordinary how ruthlessly he dealt with my father.'

'Sep was a man with exceptionally high principles,' said Maisie. She crossed the room to switch on the wireless, and paused on her way back to her chair to look down upon Edward. He was so solemn that she ruffled his thick hair teasingly.

'And a Victorian,' added Edward, still far away, 'with a good Victorian's rigid mode of conduct. It must have made life very simple in some ways. You knew exactly where you were.'

'You're going grey,' said Maisie, peering at the crown of his head, and Edward laughed.

'It's marriage,' he said, pulling her down beside him.

One morning, a week or so later, a long envelope with a Caxley postmark arrived for Edward. It was the only letter for him, but Maisie had a long one from Joan, full of news about the baby and Sarah's recovery from measles. Sipping her breakfast coffee, and engrossed in the letter from Ireland, she was unaware of the effect that Edward's correspondence was making upon him, until he pushed away his half-eaten breakfast and got up hastily.

He looked white and bewildered, and rubbed his forehead as he always did when perplexed.

'Not more bad news?' cried Maisie.

'No. Not really. I suppose one should say quite the opposite – but the hell of a shock.'

He handed her the letter and paced the room while she read it.

'He's left you *everything*?' queried Maisie in a whisper. 'But what about Aunt Kathy and your father and the other grand-children? I don't understand it.'

'They're all provided for – except for my father, which one would by incredibly large sums of money. But the two businesses are for me, evidently.'

'Didn't he ever mention this to you?'

'Never. It honestly never entered my head. It's amazingly generous, but a terrific responsibility. I thought everything would be Aunt Kathy's, with perhaps a few bequests to the others. He'd already given me the house above the restaurant. This is staggering.'

'But lovely,' exclaimed Maisie. 'Dear Sep! He always wanted you in the market square.'

Edward paused in his pacing and looked at her in astonishment.

'Do you seriously suggest that I should run the business myself? I don't know the first thing about baking – or catering for that matter.'

'You could learn,' pointed out Maisie. 'And running one business must be very like running another. And just think – to live in Caxley!' Her eyes were bright.

Edward continued to look distracted. His eye caught sight of the time and he gave a cry of dismay.

'I must be off. This will need a lot of thought. Lovejoy wants to see me anyway to sign some papers. We'll talk this over this evening, and go down again this weekend.'

'Don't look so worried,' comforted Maisie. 'Anyone would think you'd been sentenced to death! In fact, you've been sentenced to a new life.'

'Not so fast, please,' begged Edward, collecting his belongings frenziedly. 'There's a great deal to consider – Sep's wishes, the family's reactions, whether we can cope with the business ourselves or get people in to manage it properly – a hundred problems! And what about my job here? I can't let Jim down after all he's done for me.'

Maisie pushed her agitated husband through the front door.

'Tell Jim what's happened,' she said soothingly. 'And calm down. I'm going back to celebrate in a second cup of coffee.'

The day seemed to drag by very slowly for Maisie. There was no school for her that morning, and although she was glad to have some time to collect her thoughts, she longed for Edward to return so that they could discuss this miraculous news.

For her own part she welcomed a return to Caxley. To live in the market square, either in Edward's house or in Sep's, would give her enormous pleasure. Her friends were there, and the thought of living so near all her in-laws, which might daunt many young wives, did not worry Maisie who had known the Howards and Norths now for so many years. She longed too to have a sizeable house to furnish and decorate. Here, in the tiny flat, she had found small scope for her talents. It would be lovely to choose curtains and wallpaper and to bring either of the two fine old houses to life again.

And what better place to raise a Howard family than in the heart of Caxley where their roots ran so deeply? This would mean too the end of the fruitless house-hunting which depressed them both. As she went mechanically about her household tasks, Maisie hoped desperately that Edward would be able to wind up the job satisfactorily here, and return to Caxley with a clear conscience and zest for what lay ahead.

Edward returned, looking less agitated than when he had departed for the office that morning.

'Jim is as pleased as if it had happened to him,' said he. 'We've gone into things as thoroughly as we can at this stage. He's quite happy for me to go whenever I like, but we've all sorts of negotiations going on at the moment, started by me mainly, and I must see those wound up before I'd feel free.'

'And when would that be?'

'I can't say. Probably in a few months' time.'

'A few *months!*' echoed Maisie, trying to keep the disappointment from her voice.

Edward looked across at her and laughed.

'You want to go back very badly, don't you?'

Maisie nodded.

'I'm beginning to think that I do, too, but I must clear up things at this end first. We'll see what Lovejoy says at the weekend, and how the family feels. Who knows? We may be back in the market square by the New Year. That is if I've mastered the bakery business by that time!'

As they drove to Caxley that weekend, Edward had some private misgivings. How would Aunt Kathy feel about the will? She had taken an active part in the business, and it seemed hard that no share in it had been left to her. It was true that Sep's bequest to her and her children had been characteristically generous, and of a magnitude which staggered Edward, but it was not quite the same as having a part in a thriving concern. And how would the rest of the family view his amazing good fortune? Edward had seen many united families rent assunder by wills, and could only hope that the Howards and Norths would be spared this ignominy. He approached Caxley with some trepidation.

His mother and grandmother greeted them with unfeigned delight.

'Which house would you settle in, dear?' asked Mrs North with the shattering directness of old age. She refused to believe that Edward did not know yet if he would be able to return to Caxley at all.

'But you must have known, dear, that Sep intended you to have the business?'

'I hadn't a clue, grandma, and that's the plain truth.'

'Neither had I,' said his mother.

'Well, he spoke to me about it, towards the end,' maintained Mrs North trenchantly 'and I agreed that it was an excellent idea.'

'Grandma, you are incorrigible!' exclaimed Edward, amused.

'It's high time you came back anyway, to look after your mother and me. And what about your own family? Married for nearly a year and no baby on the way! It's deplorable! What you need is some invigorating Caxley air.'

Edward and Maisie exchanged delighted glances.

'Yes, grandma,' said Edward meekly.

He walked up the familiar path to Bertie and Kathy's house with a nervousness he had never felt before. Kathy opened the door to him, put her arms round his neck, and kissed him soundly. All Edward's worries fled in the face of this warm embrace.

'We're all very pleased about it,' Bertie assured him, when they were settled by the fire. 'Although Sep never said a word about his settlements we guessed that this would be the way he wanted it.'

'Would you come in with me as a partner?' asked Edward of his aunt. She smiled and shook her head.

'You're a dear to think of it, but I'm fifty-six next birthday and shall be quite glad to be away from it all. Father's left us money, as you know, and I'm glad the business is yours – still in the family, with "Howard" over the door – but not giving me any more worries.'

They talked of Edward's plans, and he explained the necessity of staying in town to clear up his affairs at the factory.

'And I'm still not absolutely sure if I ought to come back to run the shop and restaurant myself, or whether I should try and get someone to manage them.'

'John Bush and I can hold the fort until you decide,' offered Kathy. 'But *please* think about taking it on yourself. You could do it easily, and think how pleased Sep would have been.'

'And Maisie will be,' added Bertie. 'Off you go to your appointment with Lovejoy! See what he advises.'

Mr Lovejoy, pink and voluble, succeeded in confusing Edward even more, by presenting him with a host of incomprehensible documents to peruse, and a torrent of explanation.

From amidst the chaos one thing emerged clearly to Edward. He was going to be a man of some wealth. Death duties would amount to a considerable sum, but if the business continued at its present rate he could expect an income far in excess of that which he now earned. He had no doubt, in his own mind, that with some rebuilding and more modern equipment, the two businesses could become even more lucrative.

He thanked Mr Lovejoy for his help and emerged into the pale October sunlight. Hardly knowing what he was about, he passed Howard's Restaurant and crossed to Sep's old shop. It was strange to think that all this now belonged to him.

He stepped into the shop in a daze. A young new assistant, unknown to him, asked him what he would like. Edward tried to pull himself together.

'Oh, a loaf,' he said desperately. 'Just a loaf.'

She picked out a stout crusty cottage loaf from the window, shrouded it in a piece of white tissue paper, and thrust it into his arms like a warm baby.

Edward gave her a florin, and she slapped some coins into his palm in return. He studied them with interest. It was time he knew the price of bread.

Still bemused, and clutching his awkward burden, he made his way towards the Cax. What had possessed him to buy a loaf, he wondered, exasperation overcoming his numbness!

He strode now with more purpose towards the tow path. The families of mallards and moorhens paddled busily at the edge of the water, as they had always done. Today, thought Edward, they should celebrate his inheritance.

He broke pieces of the loaf and threw them joyfully upon the Cax. Squawking, quacking, piping, the birds rushed this way and that, wings flapping, streaking the water with their bright feet, as they fought for this largesse.

Exhilarated Edward tossed the pieces this way and that, laughing at the birds' antics and his own incredible good fortune. What was it that the Scriptures said about 'casting thy bread upon the waters'? He would ask Grandma North when he returned.

He thrust the last delicious morsel into his mouth, dusted his hands, and walked home, whistling.

## EDWARD MEETS HIS FATHER

The first frosts of autumn blackened the bright dahlias in the suburban gardens and began to strip the golden trees. Children were scuffling through the carpet of dead leaves as Edward drove to the factory one morning.

In his pocket lay a letter from his father. It was the first communication he had ever received from him, and it provided food for thought.

He studied it again in the privacy of his office. It was written on cheap ruled paper, but the writing was clear and well-formed. It had come from an address in Lincolnshire, and said:

My dear Edward,

Thank you for writing to tell me of the death of your grandfather.

To be frank, I had already seen a notice of it in *The Caxley Chronicle* which has been sent to me ever since I left the town.

I could not have attended the funeral, even if I had wished to do so, as the expense of the fare to Caxley made the trip impossible. I live alone here, in very straitened circumstances, my second wife having died two years ago.

I should very much like to see your mother again and, of course, you too, but I shall understand if it is not convenient. The contents of your grandfather's will are unknown to me, but I take it that he was stubbornly against me to the end.

       Affectionately,
       Leslie Howard

It was pretty plain, thought Edward, from the letter before him, that his father was as bitter as ever against Sep. Not once did he speak of him as 'my father' – but as 'your grandfather', and the final reference to the will disclosed a disappointed man. Nevertheless, Edward experienced a strong feeling of mingled pity and curiosity. His father must be getting on in years. He was certainly older than Uncle Bertie, and must now be approaching sixty. He sounded lonely too, as well as hard up.

He began to wonder how he lived. There had been two children by the second marriage, as far as he remembered. Was he perhaps living with one of them in Lincolnshire? He felt fairly certain that his mother would not wish to meet his father again, but he himself was suddenly drawn to the idea of seeing him. He turned the notion over in his mind, deciding not to do anything precipitous which might upset the family.

At the weekend, when he went once more to Caxley, he showed his mother the letter when they were alone. The vehemence of her reaction astonished him.

'He wrote to me at much the same time,' she told Edward, her face working. 'I tore up the letter. He's hurt me too much in the past, Edward. If anything, the bitterness has grown with the years. I wouldn't lift a finger to help him. He treated us all abominably, and if it hadn't been for his own father we should have been very hard up indeed. And now he has the nerve to approach us and – more than that – to expect money from Sep! The whole thing is despicable.'

It was obviously not the moment to tell his mother that he felt like visiting his father; but before he and Maisie left for home he broached the subject tentatively. He had already told Kathy and Bertie about Leslie's letter, and about the possibility of travelling to Lincoln to see how his father fared. They had both been sympathetic towards Edward's project, but had no desire to meet Leslie themselves.

'He's a charmer – or was –' said Bertie plainly, 'and a sponger. So be warned, my boy. And if your mother objects, I advise you to chuck up the idea. No point in opening old wounds.'

'I see that well enough,' responded Edward. 'But I don't like to think of him in want, when Sep has left us all so comfortably off.'

'Your feelings do you credit,' replied Bertie, 'but don't let yourself in for embarrassment in the future. Leslie might well have developed into an old-man-of-the-sea, always demanding more and more.'

As his nephew vanished up the lane to the High Street, Kathy looked at Bertie.

'Will he really go, do you think?'

'He'll go,' said Bertie. 'He feels it's his duty. He's Sep all over again when it comes to it – and the sooner we all realize it, the better.'

Luckily, Winnie's reactions to Edward's proposal were less violent than he had imagined.

'I can understand that you want to see him,' she said, rather wearily. 'He is your father after all. But I absolutely refuse to have any more to do with him. And nothing of this is to be mentioned to Grandma. She is too old for this sort of shock.'

Edward promised to be discreet, kissed his mother good-bye and drove back to London well content.

The next few weeks were unusually busy for Edward, and it was early December before the trip northwards could be arranged.

The clearing-up process at the factory was going well, but Edward was to remain one of the directors and there were a number of legal matters to arrange. Every other weekend he spent at Caxley, studying the business, and going through the accounts and staff arrangements with Kathy and John Bush. It was clear that they longed to hand over the responsibilities of the shop and restaurant which they had so bravely borne, and Edward hoped to move back to his own house as soon as the tenants in the floors below could find alternative accommodation. John Bush had been offered the little cottage where Edward and Joan had been born. A daughter, recently widowed, was to share it with him, and the old man made no secret of looking forward now to complete retirement.

Maisie was in her element choosing papers for the walls and material for curtains and covers. She went with Winnie to one or two furniture sales and acquired some fine pieces. Old Mrs North gave her the tea service which had graced her own table at the house in the market square, and Maisie liked to think of it in its own home again.

At the end of November she was delighted to discover that she was to have a baby in the early summer.

'We *must* get in before long,' she implored Edward. 'I must get everything ready for it while I'm still mobile.'

The family was as pleased as they were themselves at the news, and Mrs North's comment amused them all.

'At last,' she cried, 'we'll have a *christening* at St Peter's. Don't tell me you've anything against that?'

She was reassured, and set to work to knit half a dozen first-size vests with enthusiasm.

Edward set out alone on his journey, starting very early, as he wanted to make the return trip in the day.

It was cold and overcast when he set out, and rain began to fall heavily after an hour or so on the road. He had looked forward to this visit, but now a certain depression invaded him, due in part to the dismal weather and to general fatigue. Although he had made up his mind to return to the market square and to take up the duties laid upon him by Sep, he still had moments of doubt.

True, as Maisie had said, running one business was very like running another, but he was going to miss his trips abroad and his growing skill in designing. Life in London had been pleasant. Would he find Caxley too parochial after wider horizons? He could only hope that he was doing the right thing. In any case the thought of the baby being born in Caxley gave him enormous pleasure, and he looked forward to introducing it to all the varied delights of the Cax running through the garden.

He reached the town where his father lived a little before noon. Rain slashed against the side windows, and passing vehicles sent up showers of water across the windscreen. Wet grey-slated roofs and drab houses stretched desolately in all directions. Bedraggled people, bent behind dripping umbrellas, looked as wretched as their surroundings. Edward drove through the centre of the town and followed the route which his father's last letter had given.

He found the road, the house, switched off the car's engine and sat looking about him. It was less gloomy than parts of the town he had just traversed, but pretty dispiriting, nevertheless. The houses were semi-detached, and built, Edward guessed, sometime in the thirties. They were brick below and pebble-dash above, each having an arched porch with a red-tiled floor to it. The front gardens, now leafless, were very small. Here and there a wispy ornamental cherry tree, or an etiolated rowan, struggled for existence in the teeth of the winds which came from the North Sea.

The sharp air took his breath away as he made his way to the door. It was opened so quickly that Edward felt sure that his arrival had been watched. A plump breathless woman of middle age greeted him with an air of excitement. She wore a flowered overall and carried a duster.

'Come to see your dad?' she greeted him. 'He's been waiting for you. Come in. You must be shrammed.'

Edward, who had never heard this attractive word, supposed, rightly, that it meant that he must be cold, and followed her into the small hall. An overpowering smell of floor polish pervaded the house and everything which could be burnished, from brass stair rods to the chain of the cuckoo clock on the wall, gleamed on every side.

The door on the right opened and there stood a slight figure, taller than Sep, but less tall than Edward, gazing at him with the bright dark eyes of the Howards.

'Your son's come,' announced the woman. The words dropped into the sudden silence like pebbles into a still pool.

'Come in, my boy,' said Leslie quietly, and they went into the sitting-room together.

The meeting had stirred Edward deeply, and for a moment or two he could find nothing to say. His father was fumbling at the catch of a cupboard.

'Like a drink?'

'Thank you.'

'Whisky, sherry or beer?'

'Sherry, please.'

Edward watched his father pouring the liquid. He was very like Aunt Kathy. His hair was still thick, but now more grey than black. He had the same dark, rather highly arched, eyebrows, and the pronounced lines from nose to the corner of the upper lip which all the Howards seemed to have inherited from Sep. He was dressed in a tweed suit, warm but shabby, and his shirt was so dazzlingly white that Edward felt sure that his land-lady attended to his linen.

The room was over-filled with large furniture and numerous knick-knacks, but a good fire warmed all, and old-fashioned red wallpaper, overpowering in normal circumstances, gave some cheer on a morning as bleak as this.

'You seem very comfortable here,' ventured Edward, glass in hand.

'They're good people,' said Leslie. 'He's a railway man, due to retire soon. I have two rooms. I sold up when the wife died. Came up here from the west country, and took a job with a car firm.'

'Are you still with them?' asked Edward.

'No,' replied Leslie briefly. 'Tell me about the family.'

Edward told him all that he could. He appeared quite unaffected by Robert's tragic end and his father's recent death, but Edward noticed that mention of his mother brought a smile.

'But she won't see me, eh?'

'I'm afraid not. I hope you won't try.'

'Don't worry. I treated her badly. Can't blame her for giving me the cold shoulder now. I shan't come to Caxley. I thought of it when I read of the old man's death, but decided against it. If there were any pickings I reckoned Lovejoy would let me know.'

There was something so casually callous about this last utterance, that Edward stiffened.

'Did you imagine that there would be?' he inquired. There must have been an edge to his tone, for the older man shot him a quick glance.

'Can't say I did, but hope springs eternal, you know.'

He placed his glass carefully on the table beside him, and turned to face Edward.

'This looks like the only time I'll be able to put my side of the story, so I may as well tell it now. You knew my father well enough, I know, but only as an older man when he'd mellowed a bit. When Jim and I were boys he was too dam' strict by half. Chapel three times on Sundays and Lord knows how many Bible meetings of one sort or another during the week. Jim stuck it all better than I did – and then, as we got older, he didn't have the same eye for the girls as I had. He was more like Dad – I was like Mum. I don't think I ever loved my father. He said "No" too often.'

'But I know he was fond of all his children,' broke in Edward.

'Had a funny way of showing it,' observed his father bitterly. 'He drove me to deceit, and that's the truth. He was a narrow-minded bigoted old fool bent on getting to heaven at any cost. I can't forgive him.' He was breathing heavily.

'He was also brave, honest and generous,' said Edward levelly. His father seemed not to hear.

'And he poisoned Winnie's mind against me later. There was no hope of reconciliation while Father was alive.'

'That's not true,' said Edward, anger rising in him. 'My mother's mind was made up from the moment you parted!'

'Maybe,' replied Leslie indifferently. 'She was a North – as obstinate as her old man.' He laughed suddenly, and his face was transformed. Now Edward could see why Leslie Howard was remembered in Caxley as a charmer.

'Don't let's squabble,' he pleaded. 'We've a lot to talk over. Let's come out to a pub I know for our grub. Mrs Jones here is a dab hand with house-cleaning but her cooking's of the baked-cod-and-flaked-rice variety. I told her we'd go out'.

Edward was secretly sorry to leave the good fire and over-stuffed armchair, but dutifully drove through the relentless rain to a small public house situated two or three miles away on a windswept plain. Over an excellent mixed grill Edward learnt a little more of his father's life.

'My boy was killed in France,' said Leslie, 'and the girl is married and out in Australia.'

It was queer, thought Edward, to hear of this half-brother and sister whom he had never seen.

His father spoke of them with affection. Naturally, they were closer to him than he and Joan could ever have been.

'And then Ellen was ill for so long – three or four years, before she died. I got to hate that place in Devon. We had a garage there, you know. Dam' hard work and mighty little return for it.'

'What happened to it?' asked Edward.

'Sold everything up when Ellen went. Paid my debts – and they were plenty – and found this place. I wanted a change, and besides, the doctor told me to live somewhere flat. I've got a dicky heart. Same thing that took off my poor mum, I daresay.'

Gradually, Edward began to see the kind of life which was now his father's lot. He had fallen out with the car firm. It was obvious that he disliked being an employee after running his own business. It was also plain to Edward that if he did not have some regular employment he would very soon drift into a pointless existence in which drink would play a major part. Nevertheless, it seemed that there were grounds for believing that he had some heart complaint. The woman behind the bar, who seemed to be an old friend, had inquired about 'his attacks' with some concern, and both his parents had suffered from heart trouble.

For the past week he had been without work for the first time. He had heard of two book-keeping jobs in local firms and proposed to apply for them. Edward thought it sounded hopeful. As far as he could gather, his father's financial resources consisted of fifty pounds or so in the bank. This amount would not last long even in such modest lodgings as Mrs Jones'. This urgency to earn was a spur in the right direction, Edward surmised.

He paid the bill and drove his father home. The matter which had been uppermost in his mind was more complicated than he had first thought. He was determined to see that his father was not in want. Now that he had met him he was equally sure that this was not the time to offer financial help. If he did, the chances of Leslie's helping himself grew considerably slighter. Prudently, Edward postponed a decision, but made his father promise to let him know the outcome of his job-hunting.

'I'll write to you in a week or so,' said Leslie as they parted. 'I don't suppose we'll meet again, my boy. Better to make this the last time, I think. It was good of you to make the journey. Tell those who are interested how I am. I've got a soft spot for old Bertie. I wonder if he ever regretted marrying a Howard?'

'Never,' said Edward stoutly, driving off, and left his father laughing.

Driving back along the wet roads Edward pondered on the day's encounter. He was satisfied now that he had seen his father. He was well looked after, in fairly good health, and obviously as happy as he would be anywhere.

As soon as he heard that he was in work again he would make adequate provision against the future. He wanted to feel that there was a sum in the bank which would be available if the old man fell on hard times. But he must have a job – no matter how small the return – which would keep him actively occupied. His father's worst enemy, Edward saw, was himself. Too much solitude would breed self-pity and self-indulgence. He could see why Sep had never had much time for him. There was a streak of weakness which Sep would never have been able to understand or forgive.

'A rum lot, the Howards!' said Edward aloud, and putting his foot down on the accelerator, sped home.

# RETURN TO THE MARKET SQUARE

Edward found a surprising lack of interest in Leslie's welfare among the family. Aunt Kathy was perfunctory in her inquiries. His mother refused to discuss the matter. Maisie, naturally enough, was only vaguely interested in someone she had never met. Uncle Bertie alone seemed concerned, and listened attentively to Edward's account of all that had happened. He approved of Edward's decision to wait and see if a job materialized.

In the week before Christmas the awaited letter arrived. Leslie wrote enthusiastically. The post was in a large baker's. 'Back where I began,' was how he put it. He not only looked after the accounts but also took the van out twice a week to relieve other roundsmen. His weekly wage was modest but enough for his needs, he wrote.

Edward replied congratulating him, and telling him that he was paying the sum of two hundred and fifty pounds into his bank account which he hoped he would accept as a nest-egg and a Christmas present. He posted the letter with some misgivings. Was he simply trying to salve his conscience by handing over this money? He hoped not. What would Sep have thought? Well, maybe Sep would not have approved, but Edward had his own decisions to make now, he told himself firmly. He felt sure that it was right to supply his father with a bulwark against future storms. He felt equally sure that it had been right to wait until he was established in a suitable job before providing that bulwark. Now it was up to his father.

Everything was now planned for their removal from the flat to the market square. After innumerable delays, the old house was free of workmen and, freshly decorated, awaited its owners.

Maisie had enjoyed refurbishing the fine old

rooms. The great drawing-room, with its three windows looking out upon the market place, was painted in the palest green, a colour which would show up well the mahogany pieces which she had bought at the sales. It was a splendid room, high and airy. Bender North had always appreciated it, admiring its fine proportions and its red plush furnishings, after a day in the shop below. Now his grandson would find equal domestic pleasure in the same room.

On the same floor, at the back of the building, were the dining room and kitchen, overlooking the small garden and the river Cax. Above them were three bedrooms and a bathroom, while on the top floor, in the old attics, Edward's flat remained much as it was, except that his sitting-room had been converted into a nursery for the newcomer.

'You'll have to put the window bars back again,' said Uncle Bertie when he inspected the premises. 'There were three to each window when I slept there. You took them out too hastily, Edward my boy!'

Edward and Maisie spent the last weekend in January at Rose Lodge. She was to see the furniture in on the Monday, with Winnie's help, while Edward would return to the flat to arrange things at that end. It was bitterly cold, and as she and Winnie directed operations on Monday morning, and dodged rolls of carpet and bedsteads, Maisie was thankful that they had faced the expense of central heating for the house. With the open market square before, and the river Cax behind, it had always felt cold. Now, with new warmth, the house seemed to come to life.

She took a particular interest in the larger of the back bedrooms, for here she planned to have the baby. She was determined that it should be born in the old house in the market square, and had already engaged the monthly nurse who was to sleep in the bedroom adjoining her own.

The view from the windows on this bleak January day was grey and cheerless. The pollarded willows lining the Cax pointed gaunt fingers towards the leaden sky. The distant tunnel of horse chestnut trees made a dark smudge above the river mist, but Maisie could imagine it in May when the baby was due to arrive. Then the willows would be a golden green above the sparkling water. The chestnut leaves would be bursting from their sticky buds. The kingfisher – harbinger of good fortune – should be flashing over the water, and on the lawn below the window the crocuses, yellow, purple and white, would be giving way to daffodils and tulips.

It was past nine o'clock when Edward arrived. Both of them were excited but exhausted, and went early to bed in the bedroom overlooking the market square. Maisie fell asleep almost immediately, but Edward lay on his back watching the pattern on the ceiling, made by the lamps in the market place.

Now and again the old house creaked, as wood expanded gently in the unaccustomed heat. Someone crossed the cobbles, singing, pausing in his tune to call good night to a fellow wayfarer. There was a country burr in the tone which pleased Edward.

How often, he wondered, had Grandfather North lain in this same room listening to the sounds of the square by night? He thought of Uncle Bertie and his own mother, sleeping, as children, on the floor above, where soon his own child would be bedded. It gave him a queer feeling of wonder and pride.

Tomorrow, he told himself, he must wake early and go downstairs to the restaurant and then across to the bakery. He was a market square man now, with a reputation for diligence to keep up! Smiling at the thought, he turned his face into the pillow and fell asleep.

Caxley watched Edward's progress, in the ensuing weeks, with considerable interest. On the whole, his efforts met with approval. He was applying himself zealously to the new work, and people were glad to see a young man in charge.

The assistants in the shop and restaurant spoke well of him, and the grape-vine of the closely-knit little town hummed busily with day-to-day reports – mainly favourable. Young Edward was taking on two new counter-hands. He was going to enlarge the storage sheds at the back of the bakery. He was talking of keeping the restaurant open later at night. He was applying for a liquor licence. Think of that! The more sedate chapel-goers could imagine Sep turning in his grave at the thought, but the majority of Caxley's citizens approved.

Edward himself was beginning to enjoy it all enormously. The years of solitary living, which had been all that he desired after the break-up of his first marriage, were behind him. He began to flourish in this new gregarious life and found pleasure in joining some of the local activities and meeting boyhood friends again. The Crockfords, grandchildren of the famous Dan who had painted Edna Howard so long ago, lived within walking distance and were frequent visitors. William Crockford, the present owner of the family mill which supplied Edward with much of his flour, introduced him to the Rotary Club and Edward became an energetic member. He also took up cricket again. He sometimes went dutifully with Maisie to concerts at the Corn Exchange which she, who was musical, thoroughly enjoyed, while Edward, who was not, leant back and planned future business projects while local talent provided mingled harmony and discord.

For there was, indeed, a great deal to plan. Edward, the product of two business families, saw clearly the possibilities of the future. Times were becoming more prosperous after the lean forties. People were buying more, and demanding more luxurious goods. Caxley families were prepared to dine out in the evenings. Caxley businessmen took their lunches in the town much more frequently. What is more, they brought their clients, and talked over deals at Howard's Restaurant.

There were more cars on the road, more wayfarers travelling from London westward, and from the Midlands southward. Caxley was a convenient stopping-place, as it had been in the days of the stage-coach. The restaurant trade was booming. It could become even more thriving with judicious re-organization.

Edward was so engrossed with his present commitments and his plans for the future that a letter which arrived for him one April morning came as a bolt from the blue. He could hardly believe his eyes as he read the document.

It was from the managing director of a firm of departmental stores well known to Edward. They were proposing to set up several more branches in provincial towns. The two sites belonging to Edward would be suitable for their purpose. The larger site would be used for their drapery and furnishing departments. Their Food Hall would probably be accommodated on the present bakery site. Perhaps Mr Howard would consider taking up a position of responsibility in this department, the salary to be arranged by mutual agreement? Naturally, there was a great deal to consider on both sides, but his firm had in mind the sum of – (here followed a figure so large that Edward seriously wondered if a nought or two too many had been added) and their agents were Messrs Ginn, Hope & Toddy of Piccadilly who would be glad to hear from Mr Howard if he were interested.

Edward handed the letter to Maisie in silence.

'Well?' she said, looking up at last.

'Some hopes!' said Edward flatly, stuffing it in his pocket. 'This is ours. We stay.'

As a matter of interest he showed the letter to the family before replying to it. As he expected, Bertie wholeheartedly agreed with his decision, but Kathy and the two ladies at Rose Lodge had doubts. This surprised Edward. The two properties had been their homes and livelihoods for so long that he had felt sure that they would be as forthright in their rejection of the offer as he was himself. How strange women were!

'It's such a lot of money,' said old Mrs North. 'After all, with that amount you could start up another business anywhere, or go back to the plastics place, dear, couldn't you?'

'Or simply invest it, and have a nice little income and a long holiday somewhere,' said his mother. 'There's no need to feel tied to Caxley simply because the business has been left to you.'

'But I *want* to be tied to Caxley!' Edward

almost shouted. 'This is *our* business – the *Howard* business! Dammit all, it's the work and worry of three generations we're considering! Doesn't that mean anything?'

'Really,' tutted Mrs North, in some exasperation, 'men are so romantic about everything – even currant buns, it seems!'

'All we're trying to say,' said Winnie, more patiently, 'is that we should quite understand if you felt like accepting the offer, and I'm sure the rest of the family would agree.'

'Well, I don't intend to, and that's flat,' retorted Edward. He had not felt so out of patience with his womenfolk for years, and took a childish pleasure in slamming the front door as he departed.

He walked back through a little park, and sat down on one of the seats to cool off. Beds of velvety wallflowers scented the evening air, and some small children screamed on the swings, or chased each other round and round the lime trees. A few middle-aged couples strolled about, admiring the flowers and taking a little gentle exercise. It was the sort of unremarkable scene being enacted a hundred-fold all over the country on this mild Spring evening, but to Edward, in his mood of tension, it had a poignant significance.

Here, years ago, he had swung and raced. Before long, his own children would know this pleasant plot. These people before him, old and young, were of Caxley as he was himself. They all played their parts in the same setting, and with their neighbours as fellow-actors. And the centre of that stage was Caxley's market square. How lucky he was to have his place so firmly there – his by birthright, and now by choice as well! Nothing should make him give up this inheritance.

A very old man shuffled up to Edward's bench and sat down gingerly. His pale blue eyes watered, and a shining drop trickled down his lined cheeks into the far from clean beard which hid his mouth and chin.

His clothes were shabby, his boots broken. Edward guessed that he was making his way to the workhouse on the hill. He held a paper bag, and thrusting a claw-like hand inside, he produced a meat pasty. He gazed unseeingly before him as he munched, the pastry flaking into a shower of light crumbs which sprinkled his deplorable beard and greasy coat.

But it was not so much the old man who engaged Edward's attention as the blue and white paper bag which he held. It was very familiar to him. He had seen such bags since his earliest days – bright and clean, with 'Howard's Bakery' printed diagonally across the checked surface. Tonight, the sight of it filled him with a surge of pride. Here, he was, face to face with one of his customers, watching his own product from his own paper bag being consumed with smackings of satisfaction! Who would give up such rewards? He felt a sudden love for this dirty unknown, and rising swiftly, fumbled in his pocket and pressed half a crown into the grimy paw.

'Have a drink with it,' he said.

'Ta, mate,' answered the tramp laconically. 'Needs summat to wash this muck down.'

Edward walked home, savouring the delicious incident to the full. It warmed the evening for him. It added to his growing zest for life in Caxley, and to the enjoyment he felt, later that evening, when he pulled a piece of writing paper towards him and wrote a short, polite, but absolute rejection of the store's offer.

It was dark as he crossed the square to post it. He balanced the white envelope on his hand before tipping it, with satisfaction, into the pillar box. Now it was done, he felt singularly light-hearted, and walked jauntily back across the cobbles, smiling at Queen Victoria's implacable bulk outlined against the night sky.

At his doorway he turned to take a last breath of fresh air. The moon slid out from behind a ragged cloud, and touched the market square with sudden beauty.

Edward gave the scene a conspiratorial wink, opened his own door, mounted his own stairs and made his way to bed.

# JOHN SEPTIMUS HOWARD

It was six o'clock on a fine May morning.

The market square was deserted. Long shadows lay across the cobblestones, reaching almost to the steps of St Peter's church. At the window of his bedroom, in a crumpled suit, and with tousled hair, stood Edward. It had been one of the longest nights that he had ever known, but now peace, and the dawn, had arrived.

The monthly nurse, Mrs Porter, had been in the house with them for eight days. That she was expert in her profession, Edward had no doubt, but as a member of the household he had found her sorely trying. Her shiny red face and crackling starched cuffs and apron dominated every meal. She ate very slowly, but needed a large amount of food to keep her well-corseted bulk going, so that Maisie and Edward seemed to spend three times as long at the table.

Maisie was worried because the baby was overdue. Nurse Porter added to her anxiety by consulting the calendar daily and talking gloomily of her timetable which might well be completely thrown out by Maisie's tardy offspring. Her next engagement was in a noble household in the shires, a fact which gave her considerable satisfaction.

'And the Duchess,' she told Maisie daily, 'is

*never* late. The two little boys arrived on the dot, and the little girl was two days early. You'll have to hurry up, my dear, or the Duchess will beat you to it.'

But yesterday, when Edward returned from the shop after tea, Maisie and the nurse were in the bedroom, and all, according to Nurse Porter, was going well. Maisie's comments, in the midst of her pains, were less euphemistic.

'Shall I stay with you?' asked Edward solicitously.

'Good heavens, no!' exclaimed Maisie crossly. 'It's quite bad enough as it is, without having to put a good front on it. Go a long way away – to Rose Lodge or somewhere, so that I can have a good yell when I want to.'

Thus banished, Edward took himself to the restaurant below, and pottered aimlessly about. Thank God, he thought honestly, Maisie was not one of the modern brigade who wanted a husband's support at this time! Although he intended to stay with her had she so wished, he was frankly terrified of seeing her in pain, and squeamish at the sight of blood. Dear, oh dear, thought Edward, rubbing his forehead anxiously, what poor tools men were when it came to it!'

He had no intention of going to Rose Lodge or anywhere else for that matter, until the child was born. He would stay as close as he could while it all went on. He suffered the common terrifying qualms about his wife's safety, and to calm his agitation set himself to such mechanical tasks as sorting out the cutlery and inspecting the table linen for possible repairs.

He could settle to nothing for long, however, and walked into the little garden on the dew-wet grass beside the river, looking up at the lighted window where the drama was being enacted. Every so often he mounted the stairs quietly and listened, but there was nothing to hear. On one of these sorties he encountered the nurse, and she took pity on him.

'She's doing splendidly,' she said. 'Come and have a look.'

Maisie looked far from splendid to Edward's eyes. She looked white and exhausted, but seemed glad to see him.

'Not long now,' said Nurse Porter, with what, to Edward, seemed callous indifference to her patient's condition. 'It should be here by morning.'

'By *morning*?' echoed Edward, appalled. The hands of the clock stood at a little before two. Would Maisie live as long, he wondered desperately?

'Go and make us all a nice pot of tea,' suggested the nurse, and Edward obediently went to the kitchen to perform his task. How parents could have faced ten, fifteen and even twenty such ordeals in days gone by, he could not imagine! He decided to have a whisky and soda when he had delivered the tea-tray to his taskmistress.

Later, as the first light crept across the countryside, he dozed in the arm chair, dreaming uneasily of white boats floating upon dark water. Could they be the little boats he floated as a boy upon the Cax? Or were they the white boats 'that sailed like swans asleep' on the enchanted waters of Lough Corrib? And where was Maisie? She should be with him. Had she slipped beneath the black and shivering water? Would he see her again?

A little before five Nurse Porter woke him. Her red face glowed like the rising sun, broad and triumphant. She held a white bundle which she displayed proudly to Edward.

'Want to see your son?' she asked. 'Six and a half pounds, and a perfect beauty.'

Edward looked upon his firstborn. A pink mottled face, no bigger than one of his own buns, topped by wispy damp hair, was all that could be seen in the aperture of the snowy shawl. Nurse Porter's idea of beauty, Edward thought, differed from his own, but the child looked healthy and inordinately wise.

'How's Maisie?' said Edward, now wide awake. 'Can I see her?'

'Asleep. You shall go in later. She's fine, but needs her rest.'

At that moment the baby opened his mouth in a yawn. Edward gazed at it, fascinated. There was something wonderfully clever about such an achievement when one considered that the child was less than an hour old. Edward felt a pang of paternal pride for the first time.

'He seems a very forward child to me,' said Edward.

'Naturally!' responded Nurse Porter with sardonic amusement, and took her bundle back to the bedroom.

That was an hour ago. Since then he had seen his Maisie, well, but drowsy, drunk a pot of coffee and tried to marshal his incoherent thoughts. As soon as possible, he would telephone to Rose Lodge, but six o'clock calls might alarm the household. He must let Bertie and Kathy know too as soon as they were astir.

Meanwhile, he gazed upon the market place, pink in the growing sunlight. A thin black cat, in a sheltered angle of St Peter's porch, washed one upthrust leg, its body as round and curved as an elegant shell, and suddenly Edward was back in time, over ten long years ago, when he had stood thus, watching the same familiar scene.

What a lifetime ago it seemed! Since then he had experienced war, an unhappy marriage and personal desolation. He had watched Robert's tragic decline and death, and lost Sep, his guide and example. He had shared, with his fellows, the bitterness of war, and the numbing poverty of its aftermath.

But that was the darker side of the picture. There was a better and brighter one. He had found Maisie, he had refound Caxley, and in doing so he had found himself at last.

A wisp of blue smoke rose from Sep's old house. Miss Taggerty was making up the kitchen boiler, thought Edward affectionately. In the bakehouse, work would already have started. The little town was stirring, and he must prepare, too, for another Caxley day. It was good to look ahead. It was good too, to think that John Septimus Howard, his son, would be the fourth generation to know this old house as home.

What was it that Sep used to say? 'There's always tomorrow, my boy. Always tomorrow.'

And with that thought to cheer him, Edward went to look, once more, upon the new heir to the market square.

We very much hope you have enjoyed
this Large Print Book

If you would like to find out about
our range of other titles,
you can either enquire at your
local library or contact
the publishers by writing to us at:

Remploy Press
Lightowler Road
Hanson Lane
Halifax
HX1 5NB
or by telephone on 0422 350517

Our policy at Remploy Press is to
continually improve our product and
we would welcome any suggestion or
ideas of additional titles you may
have, from you . . . our valued readers